Christmas Boyfriend

By
S J Crabb

Contents

More books by S J Crabb

sjcrabb.com

Chapter One

I watch with fascination as the beads of sweat form on his forehead and he blinks nervously. My heart is hammering in my chest and I think I'm about to have a panic attack.

He shifts nervously in his seat and fixes me with a sympathetic look.

'It's not good news I'm afraid, Miss. Anderson. Unfortunately, we are going to have to let you go.'

I just stare at him. Both of us now locked in a staring contest as the information sinks in. Mr. Prendergast looks as miserable as I now feel. I know he is just a scapegoat; the hatchet man dealing with the dirt in the business and delivering bad news. I almost feel sorry for him - almost!

He coughs and then stares at me, his expression telling me he wants to wrap this up quickly.

I just stutter in disbelief; my voice shaky and weak. 'When?'

He clears his throat and shuffles some papers on his desk.

'Today I'm afraid. You have until the end of the day to tidy up any loose ends and say your goodbyes. I suggest you make sure everything is in place and left neatly. You will be needing a good reference and we will make sure it's a good one if you handle this in a professional manner.'

I bite back an acid retort. He must be joking. Not only have I been fired from the most mediocre job I have ever had, but he also wants me to leave quietly and with dignity. It's only 9.30 and I'll have to sit at my desk for the rest of the day putting on a brave face and acting professionally when I feel anything but.

I manage to stutter, 'Why?'

He looks at me awkwardly. 'It's Brexit, I'm afraid. It has claimed many casualties already and I'm sure you won't be the last.'

I look at him in disbelief. He has got to be kidding—BREXIT!! We're a firm of accountants for goodness' sake. We don't have one foreign customer and there's more work coming in than we can deal with; what a rubbish excuse.

He glances at the clock on the wall and looks at me with a brief expression of kindness. 'I'm sorry, Annie. If it were up to me we wouldn't be having this conversation. You're a good worker and I will be sorry to lose you.'

The tears well up as I register the kindness in his eyes. 'What am I going to do now?'

He just smiles ruefully.

'Take it on the chin and carry on. There's nothing else you can do. This is just one of those things that happen in life. Just use it to make you stronger. Dust yourself off and start job hunting. A good worker like you will soon find another job and you may be happier for it. I will always give you a good reference.'

He rummages in his desk and writes a number on a piece of paper. He colours up and blinks nervously.

'Take my number, Annie. Despite everything I want to help. If you need a reference call me. You'll be fine, I just know it.'

I smile gratefully and take the number. Pushing my seat back, I stand on shaky legs and summon up every last shred of my dignity as I say, 'Thank you, Mr. Prendergast. It can't have been easy for you either.'

I turn away, fighting back the tears. As I leave his dusty office my mind is racing. What the hell do I do now?

As I walk back to the office I think about my situation. This is a disaster. Why do companies always get rid of staff just before Christmas? Nobody is recruiting now so close to the festive season. After Christmas will be just as bad. I am now seriously screwed. I want to punch the wall and scream like a mad woman because I don't have a clue what to do next.

Instead, I reach the open office where we all sit and take a deep breath. My meltdown will have to wait; I need to get a grip and take stock of the situation.

As I walk in I notice nobody looks up. There aren't many of us and we all sit segregated behind our little-partitioned desks as we set about our work. My little cubbyhole is, as its name suggests, the worst position in the room, with the least amount of space. That doesn't surprise me. Most of the others have been here for years.

I, however, haven't even made it past the probationary period.

The room is silent and I realise that everybody already knows. There is an unnatural quiet in the room. Everyone has their heads down and look busy. Unlike the usual practice of looking busy while doing anything and everything rather than actual work. It would appear the only one who didn't know this was coming was me.

I'm quite glad about that. As I sink into my spinning chair and grab the desk to stop myself from shooting off across the room, I think about what to do next.

I stare at the computer screen and try to make sense of the jumbled thoughts crashing around my mind.

It's not fair! I've worked at Mackinlay-Sanderson for three months now. A Junior Accountant with her first step on the ladder after graduation. It wasn't the best job in the world but at least it was a start. Today my three-month probationary period is up and I was looking forward to a bit of stability in my life.

Now I'm being tossed onto the cold streets of winter to fend for myself in an unforgiving world. I don't understand why this has happened. Of everyone in the office I am the hardest worker. Most of the others just whinge and whine and do everything they can to pass the buck. I have helped each and every one of them out and tried to make a good impression.

I sigh heavily. Well, they do say, *last in first out*, and that is certainly true in my case.

Suddenly, the phone rings making me almost jump out of my skin. I soon realise that nobody is going to answer it - as usual, so just lift the receiver and say shakily.

'Mackinlay-Sanderson, Annie speaking, how may I help you?'

An irate voice shouts in my ear. 'Mr. Brown here of Ransom's Hardware. Somebody was meant to get back to me about my VAT return last week and I've heard nothing. I've got the Inland Revenue breathing down my neck for money I don't have. Now, are you going to stop filing your nails or whatever else you do with your time, young lady. After all, you sure as hell aren't working on my account, so get a move on and sort this frigging mess out.'

Feeling suddenly light-headed, I just say firmly, 'I'll just connect you to the person responsible for your account, Sir.'

He shouts. 'I thought that was you. Don't tell me you're so useless someone else has been drafted in? I knew I should have gone with Rivers and Matthews, your company is rubbish.'

With a sudden sense of freedom, I cut him off. I don't have to deal with him or his stupid VAT returns any longer. Let someone else put up with his verbal abuse for a change.

For the first time since I heard the dreaded news I feel in control. I'm not sure what's happening but the worm has turned and I've had enough. Standing up, I look around me and smile. 'Coffee anyone?'

All eyes turn in my direction. They look at me nervously and nod collectively.

I head off towards the dirty little kitchen, making a mental note to inform the Public Health Department of the bacteria-filled time bomb waiting to go off inside this building.

Feeling like a strange, revenge seeking, slightly maniacal, cartoon villain, I set about my task.

I grab the dirtiest mugs from the sink—the ones that are wallowing in a pool of dirty water from yesterday.

Without rinsing them I set them up and turn the kettle on. I rummage around in the back of the cupboard and pull out the coffee that has been in there since 2011. Then I grab the milk that has been festering in the fridge since last Tuesday, ignoring the new 'Milk of the Day.'

Then I proceed to make the rankest coffee possible for every last one of them.

Since I arrived three months ago, nobody has once offered to make me a drink. I have been the tea girl and general dogsbody to a group of people who have never made me feel welcome. I have listened to their inane stories and bent over backward to help them out at every given opportunity.

I am always the first in and last out and often work through my lunch. They give me the worst jobs and blame me when anything goes wrong. I always thought it was because I was new. You should earn your place in the office hierarchy, so I just accepted the situation and strived for excellence. Well, look where that got me.

Grabbing the biscuits that nobody likes from the cupboard, I walk back to the office balancing the tray.

First stop is Grace. A large woman, in her fifties who always looks at me with disdain. She lives with her cat and has every ailment going. In fact, she is a true study of medical science and I have had to listen politely to every detail of her many illnesses—I won't miss that.

She sees me coming and quickly picks up her phone pretending to speak to anyone rather than me. She just smiles her thanks briefly as I set the germ encrusted mug in front of her.

Next stop is Jason. Office lothario and the laziest one of all. He thinks he's a real catch and flirts his way through the working day, amid a sea of innuendo and what he thinks is flattery. It just comes across as sleazy and cringy and I'm glad I won't have to put up with him anymore. I smile as I set the mug down in front of him. He smiles and licks his lips as he studies me, with what he obviously thinks is a sexy look. Probably hoping for one last shot at a fumble against the photocopier.

'Thanks, darling, has anyone told you, you'd make someone a very sexy wife one day?'

I don't rise to him and just smile. 'Yes, my boyfriend, every day as it happens. What about you,

Jason? Have you found the woman of your dreams yet, or is she still on your Christmas wish list?'

He grins. 'I'm still looking, Annie. The trouble is, when you work with her every day and she doesn't know you exist it's hard to find someone else to measure up.'

He leans forward and stares at me creepily.

'Why don't you agree to have lunch with me and forget about that boyfriend of yours? You won't regret it, darling, I'm considered quite a catch.'

I just smile and push down the feeling of nausea that threatens to explode all over his shiny grey suit.

'Sorry, I'm a bit busy today. Maybe some other time.'

I move off before I dump the rest of the tray on his smug, sleazy face. I won't miss him at all.

Next stop is Malcolm. The oldest one here who appears to have nothing else but work in his life. He keeps his head down and just nods as I set the mug in front of him.

Of everyone, he is the rudest. He is short with me and the most unhelpful man I have ever met. He appears to hate the world and everyone in it. He deals out the worst jobs to the rest of us like a croupier in a Casino. He takes all of our ideas and passes them off as his own at the regular weekly brainstorming session with management.

Subsequently, he is in charge and has risen through the ranks with little effort on his behalf. Another one I won't miss in the slightest.

Finally, I get to Verity. Middle-aged and into eighties power dressing. She is the only woman I know who still has a perm and she still has shoulder pads in her suits. Her make-up has never changed, and she wears the highest stilettos and teeters around the office trying to look professional.

She is abrupt and cold and speaks in a put-on professional voice. Everyone is, *'Dear'*, or, *'Love'* and as far as I know she has never married. She has always treated me like an idiot and looks at me as though I'm a bad smell under her nose.

Smiling sweetly, I place the mug on her desk.

'Here you go, Verity. This should keep you going through those endless spreadsheets.'

She doesn't even smile and just nods her thanks. Cold bitch!

I resume my seat and place the mug of germs in my desk drawer. That should fester nicely by the time anyone finds it.

Now it's time to wrap this up and tie up the loose ends as instructed. The first job is to sort out my computer files.

I drag all my important ones into a file named 'Trash.' I know I shouldn't, but I appear to have lost any sense of morality as the anger takes hold. Brexit indeed. I know what this is. My three-month probationary period is up and they would have to raise my salary. They obviously do this all the time, because to my knowledge I am just another young recruit in a long line, who doesn't make it past three months. They use and abuse us and then let us go, making room for the next victim. The others are protected given the length of time they have worked here. New recruits are disposable and weak with the law firmly not on their side.

Well, I am not going quietly. Maybe they will think again next time they take someone on. It's time to make a stand.

Once the files have been hidden and coded, I set about comprising my global email to:

'All Staff.'

<u>My fellow colleagues.</u>

It is with great sadness I must inform you that I will be leaving today.

Unfortunately, Brexit has claimed yet another victim and I am off to discover the world outside these four walls.

I have enjoyed getting to know you all and will think of you fondly.

Mr. Prendergast—You are a kind and decent man. You don't deserve the rubbish they throw at you and should really consider a new job. Of everyone here you work the hardest and will be the one I'll miss the most—even though you fired me!

Grace—what can I say? You are a medical miracle and I will miss your endless tales about the state of your health. It was fascinating to hear the detailed descriptions of your many illnesses and you really are a brave soul. At least you have your cat Freddy to go home to every night. I will miss your tales of the little guy and his furball afflictions. Not to mention, the tales of his escapades throughout the day as you watch him on your cat cam via your phone. You must feel pleased that you have managed to find no information about my life, while divulging absolutely every last bit of information about your own - a true skill!

Jason—I will miss your constant attempts to get me on a date while you stare at my chest. I am sure you'll move on quickly to my replacement who may be more susceptible to your questionable charms. I'm not sure how long it will be before they find out that you do no work and just continue with your quest to discover the solution to the Rubik's cube. Btw, I mastered that in secondary school, maybe you should move onto something a little less challenging?

Malcolm—Always full of the joys of Spring and one that we can all go to for friendly words of advice and encouragement. Oops, sorry, I mixed you up with someone else I once worked for.

I have enjoyed watching you at our weekly brainstorming meetings as you take everyone's ideas and then head upstairs to management and pass them off as your own. Such an admirable skill, worthy of the promotion you seek to the coveted third-floor management suite. Carry on passing out the worst jobs to the rest of the staff while keeping the best ones for yourself, safe in the knowledge that everyone talks about you behind your back.

Verity—So professional and a real role model. In fact, everything I don't aspire to be and hope never to see again. The last three months have been such fun watching you stagger around the office in your 80s-fashion, looking down your nose at the rest of us from your 6" stilettos. Word of advice—Mason's Department Store has a fabulous personal shopper who could even drag you into the 21st century. Money well spent in my opinion.

Lastly management. Mr. Mackinlay and Mr. Sanderson. Two men who sit in their ivory tower reaping the rewards of everyone else's hard work. Making such interesting decisions, such as the one that cancelled the use of the word 'Christmas' and replaced it with 'Winter Season'. How our customers must have applauded your sensitivity to the other faiths on your annual, 'Winter Seasons' card. Oh, and not to mention your wife's charity that benefitted from your ban on sending each other Christmas cards. They must have been so grateful for the £2.50 raised. Just a heads up, while you sit upstairs congratulating yourselves on your charitable ways, the rest of your staff are organising their Christmas get together at the Pheasant. Don't feel bad that you're not invited, you probably wouldn't want to mix with the peasants, anyway.

Well, it's been good to chat, but I need to get on with the rest of my life. Three months have passed by in a flash and if it has taught me anything, it's that it was among the worse of my life. So, it is with considerable relief and immense happiness that I bid you all farewell and move on to bigger and better things.

Happy Winter Season to you all.

Annie

Chapter Two

I'm still laughing to myself, as I speedily exit the building. I pressed send and then bolted before the email hit the fan.

I don't care anymore. Our wages were paid into our banks this morning and I don't need a reference from them. Three months will easily be explained away in my CV. I could say I was writing my memoirs or something.

However, there is still the pressing matter of finding a job. Two weeks before Christmas and not a hope in hell of finding one this side of the festive season.

My phone buzzes pulling me away from my panicked thoughts and I smile as I see it's from my best friend Gail.

You up for lunch babe?

I quickly type.

Emergency! Just got fired! Meet me at Giovanni's in five?

The response is almost instantaneous.

Wtf!!! I'm on my way.

As I head towards our favourite coffee shop, I try to contain the panic setting in. Gail will know what to do. She will be the cool, calm, head of reason. My rock in my hour of need.

'Oh, my God, this is a disaster! What are you going to do, I can't think straight?'

Her words come out in a jumbled mess as she surges towards me like a tornado, her bag knocking everything off the tables as she passes them.

Ignoring the angry stares of the other patrons, she sits down and looks at me with wide, slightly crazy, eyes.

I shrug. 'I'm not sure. It's quite a shock, and I never saw it coming. I had hoped you would have a few sensible ideas.'

I fix her with a desperate look and she shakes her head.

'Not really. I could ask if there's anything going at the salon. We always need casual staff around Christmas as everyone wants their hair done.'

I smile gratefully. 'That's kind of you, but I'm not sure washing hair and sweeping up is for me. Not that I wouldn't mind doing it, in fact, I would quite enjoy it for a change. No, I need money and fast. My flat won't rent itself and its expensive living in London. My savings are non-existent and the Christmas bills have maxed out my credit card.'

We stare at each other as the realisation of my situation sinks in.

We are interrupted by my phone buzzing angrily. Looking at the display I can see it's the office calling. Even the phone sounds angry on their behalf.

Gail notices my expression and raises her eyes. 'What's happened?'

I grin mischievously and tell her every delicious detail of my revenge. By the time we have wiped our eyes and gulped down our Lattes, I feel a lot better.

Gail looks at me with a considered expression. 'So, what now?'

I sigh heavily. 'I'll head home and start looking for jobs on the web. I could use the time to get my CV up to date and strike all evidence of my time with Mackinlay-Sanderson. If I put my mind to it, I'm sure I'll find something.'

Gail smiles reassuringly. 'Of course, you will. I know, how about I pick you up later and we drown our sorrows in Divas?'

Shaking my head, I smile ruefully. 'I'd better stay in and try to sort this mess out. I should save what little money I have left, anyway. How about we meet up for coffee tomorrow instead? I may be in a better frame of mind by then.'

Gail smiles softly. 'Of course. Well, I'd better get back. I left Mrs. Abbot with a whole head of foils in. She'll be bright red instead of Auburn by the time I get back.'

She stands up to go and then grins. 'Leave it with me, honey. You know, every mover and shaker around here, head through our salon doors at one time or another. Let me put the feelers out and see if I can find you something. People love a good gossip with their hairdresser. I'm sure it will just be a matter of time.'

I look at her gratefully. 'Would you? I'd be eternally grateful.'

She laughs. 'Like I said, leave it with me. Your new job is just around the corner. I can feel it in my waters.'

As I watch her go, I try to shake the image I now have of Gail and her waters.

I head off home via the Tube. Luckily, it's not too crowded, given that it's only mid-morning. My situation buzzes around my head and I think about my predicament. I love working in the City. It has such a buzz about it and everything we need is on our doorstep.

Gail works in the nearby hair salon that I go to and we became best friends. We often head out after work and hit the West End. We have a great life and I am reluctant to let go of it so soon.

My flat is just outside London and I love living there. It's a safe-ish neighbourhood and my neighbours keep themselves to themselves. It may be small but its home and I would hate to give it up.

By the time I get home, I resolve to sort this out once and for all. As I put the key in the lock, I take comfort in being in my own space again. Finally, I can think straight.

I fire up the computer and make myself a coffee. Now for the rest of my life.

Chapter Three

Three hours later and all I've managed to do is update my CV and register with a couple of agencies.

I am interrupted by the phone ringing. As I answer it my heart leaps as I hear the welcome voice of my boyfriend, Gary.

'Hey, babe. You still on for the party tonight?'

My heart sinks. Of course, tonight is his office party and plus ones are invited. He works in an Insurance company not far from where I work, sorry worked! We met in Divas six weeks ago and he is officially now the love of my life.

I take a deep breath. 'Sorry honey, I'll have to give it a miss tonight. It's been a really bad day and I'm in no mood to party. You go though.'

He sounds annoyed. 'Why, what's happened? I've told everyone you're coming now and I'll look like an idiot.'

I swallow hard as I voice the words that have caused my life to change so quickly.

'I got fired today and the last place I want to be is an office.'

Just for a minute there is silence and then he says softly. 'I'm sorry, babe. What happened?'

I sigh heavily. 'My probationary period was up and so was I it would seem. I was about to get expensive so they cut costs and terminated my temporary contract. Typical Accountants!'

He sounds annoyed.

'Well, don't let the bastards get you down. Come out with me and we'll get roaring drunk and do unspeakable things when I take you home to my bachelor pad.'

Despite myself I grin. Hm, may not be such a bad idea. A drunken night out with the man of my dreams followed by a night of unbridled passion, sounds good to me.

I almost relent but then see yet another recruitment site flashes up on Google.

'Sounds great but I'll have to pass. You go and I'll see you tomorrow instead. I may be in a better mood by then.'

'Well, I'm disappointed, babe, but I understand. I'll have a word with my boss. Maybe they could use your skills in our accounts department. It would be good to work together. We could indulge in illicit pursuits in the stationery cupboard during the working day.'

I laugh. Gary always cheers me up.

'See you tomorrow Romeo and have fun. Make sure you get a cab home. I know you and your friends. The bar will be dry within minutes with you lot around. Just stay safe and try not to have too much of a hangover when you pick me up tomorrow.'

He laughs. 'Love you, honey. Don't work at it too hard. Something will come up and if it doesn't, there's always tomorrow when we meet up.'

He laughs and I grin as I hang up. Gary is just what I need right now. Somebody fun to take my mind off my situation. Anyway, pushing him from my mind I set about the thankless task before me.

By the end of the day all I've achieved is discovering there's no job with my name on it.

I grab a salad from the fridge and eat it while staring morosely at the news. I may have to take Gail up on her offer at the salon. Something will be better than nothing, and it will tide me over until the New Year.

Feeling better about the one decision I've made that may bring in some money, I think about Gary and the party.

Maybe I should go. He's right, they may need some help in their accounts department, or anywhere else come to think of it. Burying myself away in my flat isn't going to get me a job. I need to network, get out there and meet and greet. This will be the perfect opportunity.

Two hours later I am standing outside Gary's office block. All around me people are milling around, either heading out to the many bars that surround the office complex or attending their own Christmas parties.

Despite being cold it's a lovely evening. London always looks magical at night and the stars are out clearly tonight. The air is crisp and cold and I pull my coat around me tightly and hurry inside.

Minster Insurance is located on the fifth floor. As I wait for the lift, I look around me with interest. This building is modern and sleek. It homes many companies within its walls and I could picture myself working here.

Maybe I will come back tomorrow and find out more about the companies here. I could chat to the receptionist and pick her brains. I must be proactive in looking for a job; sitting around in my flat won't pay the bills.

The lift arrives and I join a group of party goers as we cram inside its metal walls.

The guy next to me looks at me appreciatively and I pull my coat tighter around the little black dress that I'm wearing. My hair is curled and sits piled on top of my head and my makeup is heavy to withstand the evening ahead.

He shifts closer and I shrink against the walls. He smiles and I see a spark ignite in his eyes as his gaze travels the length of me. He says in a deep voice.

'Hi, are you looking for Matthews and Finch?'

I shake my head.

'No, Minster Insurance. My boyfriend is waiting for me there.'

My words don't faze him and he just grins. 'Well, if you don't find him, then head up to our party. We're on the 6th floor, 3rd door from the right. I'll buy you a drink if you like.'

I just smile and look down. 'Thanks, but I'll be fine.'

He shrugs, then luckily the lift arrives at my floor and I exit quickly before he can say another word. Maybe working here wouldn't be such a good idea.

Chapter Four

Gary's office is heaving. The noise is tremendous and as office parties go, this one appears to be a good one. Unlike Mackinlay-Sanderson, these people obviously know how to have a good time.

There are Christmas decorations everywhere. They obviously don't have a problem with Christmas cards because there are lots of them, scattered around desks and pinned to noticeboards.

The music is thumping loudly and I almost can't hear my own thoughts. It would appear there are many people that work here, judging by the number of bodies squeezed into the large office space. I know that 'plus ones' were invited, but even so, this place is crammed.

I crane my neck to look for a familiar face but immediately draw a blank. Somebody pushes past me and I stumble. Just as I think I'll embarrass myself by falling to the ground, a strong hand reaches out to steady me. I look at my rescuer gratefully and find myself staring into the eyes of a guy who looks about my age.

He grins and I feel him checking me out.

'Hey. I haven't seen you before, do you work here?'

I shake my head and shout, trying to make my voice heard above the music.

'No, I'm here with someone but appear to have lost him.'

He rolls his eyes. 'Typical. All the good ones are already taken. Who is he, maybe I can help?'

'Gary Marshall!'

He laughs. 'That figures. Gary's always had a lot of luck with the ladies.'

I feel annoyed at his words. I know Gary's good looking and a bit of a flirt, but he's a good boyfriend. He may have once played the field, but not anymore.

He obviously senses my disapproval because his face softens and he smiles apologetically.

'Well, he's one lucky guy. Come on, I'll help you look for him. Shouldn't be too difficult because if I know Gary, he will be hugging the makeshift bar area.'

I smile at him gratefully. Despite first impressions, he seems quite nice really, so I follow him further into the crowd.

The music is loud so we shout to be heard. He pushes through the heaving masses and leads me to the end of the room. A group of desks have been pushed against a wall and are groaning under the weight of a small off-licence.

'What are you drinking?!' He shouts, grabbing a plastic cup from the desk.

'Red wine, if you've got it!'

I watch as he pours a large amount of wine into the cup and thrusts it towards me before grabbing a beer from the plastic ice-filled crate underneath.

He smiles and clinks my drink with his.

'Cheers.'

I smile and take a large gulp of wine. This is surprisingly good wine, not the usual petrol that gets served at these things.

He looks at me and smiles and I notice how attractive he is. Tall, quite well built, with dirty blonde hair and a wicked grin. If I wasn't so in love with Gary he would be very much my type.

'So, how long have you been with Gary?'

I smile back at him. 'Six weeks. We met in Divas.'

He laughs. 'Of course, you did. Gary loves that place; he really should have shares in it.'

I look at him curiously. 'What about you, what do you do here?'

He rolls his eyes. 'Sorry, where are my manners? My name's Alex and I run this office for my sins. I'm in charge of the claims department; it's my job to keep these unruly guys in check.'

I raise my eyes. 'It would appear you have your work cut out then.'

He laughs as a guy falls against the table and sends the plastic cup tower crashing to the ground. He hiccups and then stumbles off without another word.

Alex grins and picks the cups up.

'They're allowed a one-night pass at the annual office party. The rest of the time I rule over them with a rod of iron.'

I laugh. 'I don't doubt that for a second.'

He grins. 'So, what about you? What do you do when you're not running around after Gary?'

I sigh heavily. 'I'm an accountant - between jobs, as of today.'

He raises his eyes. 'Why, what happened?'

I shrug. 'Three-month probationary period came to an end, and I was yet another casualty of Brexit.'

He snorts. 'And you believe that, do you?'

I roll my eyes. 'Of course not. I know how it all works and Brexit was just a convenient excuse. They have a revolving door when it comes to probationers and I should have seen it coming. I'm just going to have to be smarter next time.'

He looks concerned. 'If you give me your number, I could enquire here for you?'

I smile at him thankfully. 'Sure, that would be very kind of you. I need all the help I can get at the moment. It would appear there isn't much call for accountants this side of Christmas.'

I rummage around in my bag and pull out a squashed business card. I had these printed when I was job hunting; thank goodness I still have 2000 of them. I have a feeling I will need every one.

He looks at the card and smiles. 'Well, Anne Anderson, I'm very pleased to meet you. My name is Alex Carstairs and I will do my utmost to assist you in your quest for employment.'

I shake his outstretched hand and grin. 'I'm pleased to meet you too, and thank you kind sir, all offers of help are gratefully received.'

We just grin at each other and then I remember that I'm here to find Gary. I look around to see if I can spot him.

'You know, Alex, I still can't see Gary anywhere, do you think he's even here?'

He shrugs. 'I saw him earlier. He could have slipped out I suppose. Oh, there's Alan his partner in crime, he'll know where he is. After all, they are usually joined at the hip.'

Once again, I follow him into the crowd and try to stop my wine from spilling as we crash into the sea of bodies all around us.

Finally, we stop in front of Alan; at last, a familiar face. He is obviously quite drunk already because his eyes are red and he looks at me as if I'm a stranger.

Alex shouts. 'Have you seen Gary anywhere?'

Alan shakes his head in confusion and slurs.

'He's around here somewhere.'

He blinks and then looks at me carefully as though he can't quite place me. Then the realisation hits and he looks surprised.

'Hey, Annie, I thought you couldn't make it.'

I shake my head and smile. 'I changed my mind. I thought it better than wallowing in my dilemma at home, after all, it is Christmas, the season to be merry.'

He shakes his head and if I'm honest looks slightly worried.

Alex looks at him thoughtfully and then a rather inebriated woman presses herself against him.

'Alex honey, I've been looking for you everywhere. Come and dance with me.'

She then proceeds to rub herself against him, gyrating like she's in a scene from Dirty Dancing. My goodness, the workers here certainly know how to party. I couldn't imagine doing that to Mr. Prendergast. Mind you, if he looked like Alex I may be tempted.

Alex reaches out and very firmly pushes her away and smiles.

'Come on, Fiona, let's find Tony. I'm sure I saw him looking for you over by the photocopier.'

He grins at me and rolls his eyes. 'I'll leave you with Alan. If anyone can find Gary he can. It was good to meet you, Annie.'

I smile gratefully. 'Thanks, Alex, have a happy Christmas.'

He grins and pockets my card. 'You too. Hopefully, I'll be in touch regarding a job in the New Year. Maybe Santa will be kind to you.'

I nod. 'Let's hope so. Like I said, it appears I need all the help I can get.'

I watch as he guides a very drunk Fiona through the crowd. Gosh, what a nice boss he is. Gary is lucky to work for him.

I turn back to Alan but find he is nowhere to be seen. What? How did I lose sight of him so quickly?

I look around, but it's as if he's melted into the floor. Where is he?

Sighing, I start scanning the room. Surely, it's not too difficult to find him in here.

Ten minutes later and I still haven't found either of them. All around me couples are having a great time and there is much laughter and lots of smooching. Chance would be a fine thing.

Suddenly, I spy Alan again, pressed up against some girl near the wall. I keep my eyes on him and walk with determination towards them.

Tapping him on the shoulder, he looks around and his face falls.

'Oh, Annie, sorry, haven't you found Gary yet?'

I shake my head as his date, for want of a better word, looks at me curiously. 'Are you looking for Gary?'

I nod and she goes to speak, but Alan jumps in and throws her a strange sort of warning look.

'I think he's gone, Annie. I saw him leave ten minutes ago. I thought you'd found him and were heading off. Maybe he's gone to Divas.'

His partner looks surprised and looks between us before looking down to the floor.

A feeling of uneasiness creeps over me. I'm not stupid. Alan is covering for Gary and I don't know why.

Suddenly, the music stops and somebody shouts. 'Sorry guys, can I just have your attention for a minute.'

We look over and I see Alex standing on a chair at the end of the room.

'I'll make this short as I don't want to cut into your drinking time. I just wanted to say thanks for all your hard work this year. Our targets were met, and we came out among the top in the company. You're a great team and can expect a bonus in your pay. Now enjoy tonight and don't get too drunk and get home safely. Have a lovely Christmas and let's make next year even better.'

He raises his glass and as he does so the distinct sound of the tune of Hawaii-5-O chimes through the office.

I know that sound—it's Gary's ringtone. It appears to be coming from the door next to me. I just have time to register the panic in Alan's eyes before I yank the door open. It reveals Gary with his trousers around his ankles. He is pressed into a girl with her dress bunched up around her waist and her legs wrapped firmly around his.

The office is silent as we witness the two-people going at it, in what appears to be the stationery cupboard.

Just for a second time stands still. I watch in shock, my boyfriend and the love of my life, getting it on with another in front of the entire office. Suddenly, the girl's eyes open and she utters a small shriek into Gary's mouth and pushes him away. He looks around in confusion and registers the fact that the whole office is watching him. Then his eyes settle on mine.

Panic fills them and he looks at me with confusion as he whispers, 'Oh my God, Annie!'

Pain fills my heart, quickly followed by anger. You have got to be KIDDING me!!

The anger takes hold and I do the first thing I can think of. Stepping forward, I throw the contents of my plastic cup all over his cheating, lying, despicable, face. Then I turn around and make my way out of the office, through the stunned crowd and out of the most humiliating experience of my life—so far.

Chapter Five

I almost run to the lift. This can't be happening. I actually think this is the worst day of my life, ever! I can feel the tears welling up and will myself not to fall to pieces before I make it home.

I frantically press the call button and silently pray for it to hurry before Gary finds me—if he tries that is.

Finally, after what seems like forever, the lift arrives and I race inside, my heart pounding.

The doors begin to close but just before they do, they are forced open and somebody pushes their way inside.

I look up into the extremely kind, compassionate eyes of Alex. As the doors close, he looks at me kindly. 'I'm sorry, Annie, that was horrible.'

I shrug miserably. 'Don't be. At least everything bad is happening on the same day. I'm glad to have found out now rather than wasting a minute more on that lecherous asshole.'

He laughs softly and then looks at me with concern. 'What now?'

I shrug. 'I'll go home and try to get some sleep. Tomorrow I'll consider my options. One thing's for sure, I now have no job and no boyfriend. I just need to work on the possibility of having no home unless I get a job and fast.'

He looks sympathetic. 'Let me buy you a drink. Maybe we can come up with something between us?'

I smile sadly. 'That's kind of you, Alex, but I think I'll just head off home. It's been a long, exhausting day and I need to be on my own.'

The lift arrives at the ground floor and he looks at me with concern. 'How will you get home?'

I shrug. 'I think the Tube's still running, I'll just grab that. It's only three stops and a five-minute walk at the other end. I'll be fine.'

He shakes his head. 'I'm not happy about that, Annie. With your luck today, something is bound to go wrong and I would never forgive myself. I'll call you a cab from a reliable company we use. My treat.'

Tears pool in my eyes at his words. He is so kind, and it makes me crumble. He sees my imminent meltdown coming and pulls me towards him, rubbing my back gently.

'Let it all out, Annie. Cry all you want and then dry your tears and move on. It may seem bad now, but you will look back at this and be grateful that it happened. There's a much better future for you out there, I just know it.'

The doors close again and we start heading back up the way we came. It doesn't matter though. I just go along for the ride, clinging onto the kind stranger who is obviously my guardian angel sent to me in my hour of need. In fact, I would ride this lift all night just to feel safe against the world at this moment. Just for the next few short minutes it's not just me and my problems. I am protected in a lift bubble with the kindest man I have ever met and I never want this moment to end.

I think we ride up and down in the lift for a good half an hour. No words are necessary. Alex holds me and I sob on his shoulder. Sometimes the lift stops at a floor, but when faced with the scene in front of them nobody gets in.

Fleetingly it occurs to me that this could be some kind of new therapy. Maybe I could market it as, 'Lift Therapy.' I could make it my new business and just hire out Alex's to provide comfort in people's hours of need.

By the time we reach the ground floor, for the tenth time, I feel better.

Pulling back, I look at Alex gratefully.

'Thanks, Alex, you've been so kind. I'd better let you get back to the party.'

He smiles and shakes his head. 'Come on, I'll get you that cab.'

We walk in silence, through the reception area and out into the frosty night. Despite the late hour London is heaving. It really comes alive at night and transforms into a magical land of excitement. The lights illuminate the grand buildings and the River Thames twinkles in the light. All around is laughter and despite my predicament it lifts my spirits. I will get through this dark time. Alex is right, it was meant to happen to make way for a better life. Now I just need to discover what that is.

Alex escorts me to the cab office he uses and makes sure I'm safely inside. He pays the driver and I tell him my address. Just before we go he smiles gently at me.

'It was good to meet you, Annie. Stay strong and keep focused. I'll put the word out regarding the job. Just try to have a great Christmas and put all this behind you.'

I nod gratefully. 'Thanks, Alex, you've been so kind. I hope that Santa is good to you this year because you deserve it.'

He pulls out his card and offers it to me.

'Call me after Christmas. I want to know how you get on.'

I smile shakily. 'I will. Thanks again, I really mean that.'

He grins and then closes the door. As the driver pulls away, I wave to him until he disappears from view. What a great guy.

The next morning, I meet up with Gail at Giovanni's as arranged. She looks at me in disbelief as I relay the events of last night.

'He did WHAT?!!' Gail looks at me in shock as I nod miserably.

'It was horrible, Gail. Seeing the man I love inside another will stay with me forever.'

She reaches out and grabs my hand. 'The slime-ball. Don't worry, you're obviously better off without him. You always were too good for him and you know it.'

Despite how I'm feeling, I grin.

'Yes, you're right. Who needs him anyway?'

As if on cue my phone rings and I see Gary's name flash up on the screen.

Gail looks at me and rolls her eyes.

'That's the tenth time he's called since we've been sitting here. Are you going to speak to him?'

I shake my head. 'No, he's not worth my time.'

As it rings off, I change the contact details on my phone and type in my new name for him with a flourish.

'There. From now on he will be known as 'Tosser'!'

Gail laughs and we giggle as the phone rings again, flashing his new name up on the screen. She laughs.

'Why don't you just delete him?'

I shake my head. 'No, because then I may answer it by mistake. This way I can see it's him and take great satisfaction in ignoring it.'

She nods in agreement. 'I see your point. So, what now? I mean, as Christmas's go this is turning into the one from Hell.'

Sighing, I pick up my coffee and contemplate my future.

'I think Alex was right when he told me that bad things may still happen, given the way my luck is heading.'

Gail looks confused. 'What do you mean?'

I sigh irritably. 'Well, they say that bad things always happen in threes. First, I lost my job and then my boyfriend cheated on me. The third thing may mean I'm forced to give up my flat. I'm paid up for the next three months and if I don't find a job in that time, I'll be homeless as well.'

Gail looks annoyed. 'No, you won't. If that happens you can crash with me. I told you I'll find you a job and if I can't then it sounds like Alex may. He sounds gorgeous by the way. What about him, he may be your new guy? He seems to really like you already, so obviously has extremely good taste.'

I smile at the thought of Alex. 'Yes, he's certainly a great guy and rather good looking as it happens. The trouble is, I'm not looking to replace Gary quite so soon. Maybe I'll just keep him as a friend and then, who knows?'

Gail nods in agreement. 'So, what are your plans now? You can come home with me if you like?'

I shake my head gloomily, once again sinking into the depression that is never far away.

'No. I'm afraid there is really only one option open to me now.'

She raises her eyes. 'Which is?'

I groan in despair. 'Unfortunately, things are about to get a whole lot worse. I'm going to have to go home for Christmas.'

Chapter Six

I sit back in my seat and look around me with a sinking feeling. Here I am on a train heading to Dorset to spend Christmas with my family. Most people would be looking forward to spending quality time with their nearest and dearest. Not me though, it's an ordeal that I could well do without.

To make matters worse, the only ticket I could buy was in First Class. It seems that everyone is heading to the West Country this weekend, and it was the only one available. The amount I had to pay has depleted my ever-decreasing funds even further, which has irritated me even more than I was in the first place.

The train hasn't even left London yet and I'm dreading the journey. Two hours to wallow in my own self-pity with nobody to talk to. Leaning my head against the window, I feel my depression rushing to the fore.

I hear the whistle and the doors close. Oh well, no turning back now. Two hours to get my story straight because the truth is not an option.

As we pull away, I look out of the window and sigh heavily. Christmas with the family, this I could so do without.

I am distracted from my thoughts as I see a man heading down the aisle towards me. There's an empty seat opposite me with a table in between. I note that he appears angry as he looks around him with irritation.

Great, two hours sitting opposite Mr. Angry; my luck!

There are lots of other people in the carriage, but they are all with other people and their chatter fills the air. There's a couple who hold hands and gaze into each other's eyes.

A large couple are eating some sort of sandwich and appear to have set up a picnic on the table across the aisle from me. Luckily, there are no children. That would be just my luck, a screaming brat running up and down the carriage for two hours.

I try not to look at the angry man as he thrusts his case into the overhead compartment and sits down heavily in the seat opposite. Eye contact is strictly forbidden on British Rail. It's the British way. No conversation, just polite smiles, and disapproving looks to anyone with the audacity to raise their voice. No, the best way to survive the train is to either read or look out of the window. You need to be aware of your fellow passengers at all times and do everything possible to avoid conversation.

As we head off I just lean my head against the window and stare at the scenery as it rushes by.

My family is a nightmare! I'm just glad they live in Dorset and I'm spared from mixing with them. If I'm lucky, I only get to see them about four times a year. Christmas, Easter, mum's birthday and the annual summer holiday. I hope they are distracted and I can just hide on the beach somewhere. Despite the cold, it would be the best place to be—away from them and their extremely mad ways.

The gentle hum of the engine and the gentle rocking of the train soon causes my eyes to close. The heat in the carriage and the inactivity causes my eyelids to droop and soon I am in a land where my problems don't exist. If only I could stay there through Christmas and wake up with a fantastic new job and a boyfriend who doesn't cheat on me.

Soon the noise subsides and I am in blissful ignorance of my situation.

I'm not sure how long I sleep for, but it feels almost instantaneous when the shrill ringtone of my phone wakes me.

I blink and sit up, staring around me in confusion and can see my phone resting on the table in front of me. Suddenly, I'm aware of the rather amused smirk of angry man as he looks at me.

Looking down, I can see what he finds funny. 'Tosser,' is plain for all to see and is shouting for attention via the vibrating phone on the Formica table top. Grabbing the phone quickly I press reject, registering the satisfaction that I get every time I reject him.

I can feel my cheeks burning as I see the amused face of the man in front of me, and just offer a small smile and resume looking out of the window. Phew, potential conversation averted.

A quick glance at my phone shows that I was only asleep for ten minutes. Oh, for goodness' sake, trust Tosser to ruin things for me. He is even messing with my sleeping pattern.

I decide to grab my book from my bag and try to read a few pages. Usually I read on my phone, but knowing Tosser he would ruin that too. Putting the phone on silent, I reach into my bag and pull out Fifty Shades.

I am interrupted from the secrets of Christian Grey's red room by the drinks cart rolling down the aisle.

Maybe a coffee will keep me awake. Angry man appears to be polishing something technical opposite me. It looks like a camera lens, but what do I know? All my photos are taken on my iPhone these days. At least there are several filters on there and photoshop to disguise the real me.

I purchase a cup of British Rail coffee and instantly regret my extravagance. Nobody in their right minds like what they serve. They just buy it for something to do. Typical British really. The weather is so bad we just drink tea all day and talk about what type of rain is falling. The one I can moan about for hours is that fine rain that drenches you through without you knowing.

As soon as I take my first sip, I regret it. Disgusting! I will need at least three sugars to make that drinkable.

Putting it down on the table, I flick through my book again.

I suppose I must read for another thirty minutes when disaster strikes. The train lurches and causes me to fall forward. As I do I knock the table and watch with dismay as the now cold, hideous cup of coffee, empties itself all over angry man's lap and pre-mentioned lens. I watch with horror as he jumps up, and the coffee runs off him like the River Thames.

My hands fly to my face in shock and I jump up, apologising profusely as I go.

'I'm so sorry, please let me help you.'

He glares at me angrily and I do the only thing that I can think of and start tearing the pages from my book in a vain attempt to mop up the dark brown liquid.

He glares at me angrily and snaps. 'Just leave it, it'll be fine.'

I sink back in my seat as he glares angrily at me and say in a quiet voice.

'Please, let me pay for any damage. I'm so clumsy, I didn't mean to do that.'

He looks irritated and barks. 'I said it's fine.'

He thrusts the lens into his bag and then pulls out a hip flask. I watch in amazement as he unscrews the cap and takes a long slug of whatever is in there. Wow, he's obviously read, Girl on a Train and packed accordingly.

He sees me staring and just for a second his mouth twitches and he holds the flask out towards me.

'Here, you look as if you could use this as much as me.'

I squeak. 'What do you mean?'

He smiles and for some reason my heart rate increases. Now the angry face has gone, it has been replaced by an extremely handsome one. Come to think of it, this man is gorgeous. How did I not notice that before?

He has short, slightly spiky dark hair and piercing blue eyes. He has a shadow of stubble on his face and his clothes are what I would describe as urban chic. Smart jeans and T-shirt with a casual jacket. He is also wearing those man bracelets and has a leather necklace slung casually around his neck. All in all, he looks cool and edgy and spells trouble on every level.

Tentatively, I reach out and take the flask. Raising it to my lips, I take a deep breath first. Brandy, if I'm not mistaken. He stares at me with interest as I take the smallest sip known to man. Not because I want the drink, but perversely because I want my lips where his have just been.

Damn Fifty Shades - why didn't I bring Hello Magazine instead? I hand it back and he looks at me with interest.

'So, tell me, what's your story?'

I look around me feeling uncomfortable. Doesn't he know it's against the law to engage with strangers on a British train?

I shrug. 'Just heading home for Christmas. What about you?'

He looks irritated again.

'A wedding for my sins. Tried everything to get out of it, but they dragged me into it in the end.'

I smile and he holds the flask out to me again.

'Here, have some more. You look as fed up as I am. Maybe we can help each other pass the time, on this tedious train to Hell.'

I take a sip and feel the burning liquid racing down my throat, leaving a warm feeling inside. Maybe I should chat with this sexy, gorgeous stranger. The fact that he may be trying to get me drunk, before murdering me is of no consequence.

I smile as I hand back the flask. 'Weddings are supposed to be fun.'

He pulls a face. 'Not this one. Unfortunately.'

Now I'm interested. After all, what can be so bad about going to a wedding?

I watch as he takes a large slug of brandy and then leans back in his seat, sighing heavily. He nods towards the ruined lens in his bag.

'I'm a photographer for my sins. Not your usual wedding one, more fashion. The wedding is my cousin Charlotte's and the man she is marrying is one of the vilest men I have ever met. She can't see what an idiot he is and the last thing I want is anything to do with the whole thing.'

I hand him the flask back after taking a larger gulp than usual. As the liquid burns within me, I feel all warm inside. I absolutely must get me one of these. Everything seems so much better now than it did five minutes ago.

I smile and lean forward on the table.

'We all make strange choices in life, me too as it happens. Sometimes we discover our mistake quickly, other times it takes a while. If he's as wrong as you say, then she will find out. Or it could be you know nothing about their relationship at all. He may be the sweetest guy in the world to your cousin and you should trust her judgement. I mean, what woman in her right mind would marry a total pig?'

He laughs and then leans forward. Suddenly, his face is just inches from mine and I can smell the intoxicating smell of his aftershave, mingled with the rich tones of the brandy. He whispers, 'Tell me about Tosser. Was he a mistake?'

I laugh and grab the flask from him and take a long, deep, slug. Suddenly, my inhibitions have completely left the building and I lean further forward and whisper.

'Last seen very much inside some girl at his office party, copulating in the stationery cupboard. I think I've had a lucky escape, don't you?'

He grins. 'Sounds a keeper.'

I lean back and break the spell. This man is starting to affect me and what with the effects of the alcohol, I'm liable to totally embarrass myself at any minute. Time to get a grip.

'So, what will you do about the wedding photographs? I've ruined your camera. Maybe it will be your excuse?'

He also leans back and shrugs dismissively.

'I've got others. No, my main problem isn't the photography.'

'What is it then?'

He looks irritated. 'It's the fact that the place will be riddled with my family and other animals. A whole weekend with them and I'll need several more of these just to make it to Christmas.'

I nod in agreement. 'Tell me about it. I also feel your pain. The fact that I'm heading home at all shows you how desperate I am. My family are complete nut jobs and I must have been temporarily without my sanity when I rang them and told them I was coming home for Christmas. I should have just stayed in my flat and wallowed in self-pity while watching Christmas TV. It would be much more fun than Christmas in Dorset.'

He laughs. 'Tell me about your family.'

I grin. 'I'll give you the edited, stranger version. Mum and Dad run a holiday let business on the outskirts of Dorchester. I have one sister, Gina, who as we speak is making her way there with her latest boyfriend. He's a detective, and she works as a Scene of Crimes officer. Apparently, it was love at first sight over a mutilated murder victim.

Subsequently, my mum is getting very excited that he may be, 'The one.' My gran is also booked in, which scares me the most. Totally unconventional and poles apart from my mother. Sometimes, I think mum was adopted because two more different people you couldn't wish to find. My Auntie Rose is coming with her six-year-old twin boys. Her husband is away at sea on the oil rigs, or at least that's what he tells her.'

He smiles. 'They don't sound so bad.'

I laugh loudly and notice the strange looks of our fellow passengers. Oops, I forgot the don't draw attention to yourself rule.

'I told you, I gave you the stranger version. The reason I'm dreading it so much is that my mum will fawn over the new boyfriend and Gina will take every opportunity to rub in the fact that she has found love and once again I have not. I am always the one on my own and she teases me with tales of my imaginary boyfriends.'

He raises his eyes. 'Imaginary boyfriends?'

I laugh, a little more quietly this time.

'When we were young I used to have imaginary friends. In fact, I had a whole gang of them just to annoy her. Gina was popular at school and had many friends. I never did, so I made them up. Then we progressed to boys, and it was no different. Once again, I made them up and nobody ever saw them—obviously. I thought my luck had changed when I met Tosser. He was good-looking and funny and appeared to really like me. Finally, I could brag about someone real and boy did I.

Now I'm heading home to more jokes about my imaginary boyfriend while being presented with my sister's latest conquest. I will probably have to spend the whole time walking the dog and entertaining the children.'

He looks interested and I can see his mind working. Just for a few minutes we sit in silence. The brandy is starting to take effect and my eyes start to close as the movement of the train and the heat in the carriage set to work.

I must fall asleep or pass out because the next thing I know I wake up face down on the Formica table. As the carriage swims into view, I look around me bleary-eyed and notice the disapproving stares of the other passengers. Looking over to my stranger danger I see him looking totally sober and looking at me with amusement.

'Nice sleep?'

Wiping some dribble from my mouth, I sink back into my seat with embarrassment and laugh softly.

'Sorry - was I snoring?'

He laughs. 'No, you looked quite cute really. I think your bag's been buzzing though.'

I start rifling through my bag and pull out my phone. Twenty missed calls from Tosser and five texts. Two from my mum and three from Gail.

Noticing the display, he grins.

'Popular, aren't you? You may want to keep those notifications to prove they're not from imaginary friends.'

I thrust the phone back in my bag and sigh.

'The trouble is, except for my friend Gail, I have no interest in any of them.'

Suddenly, he leans forward and whispers.

'Listen, while you were sleeping, I had an idea. I mean, say no if you want to, I would completely understand, but how about you and I helping each other out?'

I look at him in confusion.

'What are you talking about?'

He smiles wickedly. 'You need a boyfriend and I need a girlfriend. You help me out and I you, no strings attached. It will make Christmas a lot more fun for us both and get one over on our families at the same time. We will know the real situation, but they won't. What do you say, are you up for a game of deception this Christmas?'

Just for a second, I stare at him in total shock. Then I pinch myself—I mean, really, I do. I shake my head slowly.

'I'm sorry, but did I wake up? I think you just propositioned me after trying to get me drunk. You could be a murderer or a rapist and I should pull the alarm cord immediately while screaming for help.'

He just laughs and fixes me with his gorgeous eyes.

'So, what do you say, you up for a laugh?'

I grin slowly. 'Of course, I am. It will be fun— boyfriend!'

Chapter Seven

By the time the train arrives we have our story straight. My new boyfriend is called Liam Goodwin and as he said is a photographer. We met in London at Divas and have been inseparable ever since. We decided to stick as close to the truth as possible to prevent me from slipping up.

We've been dating for two months and it's getting serious. I must accompany him to the wedding as his girlfriend, which will give him the perfect excuse to spend as little time with his family as possible.

Then we will head back to my parents, where he will play the perfect boyfriend before being called back to London. There you go, a few days of madness and a lot of 'I told you so's.' Dignity intact and face very much saved.

He didn't object when I took a photo of him on my iPhone and forwarded it to Gail, for security's sake. After all, he may really be a murderer or something.

So, here I am in a taxi speeding away from Dorchester railway station towards the country home that is the wedding venue. Luckily, I have my

Christmas dress in my luggage so will be good to go.

Liam has promised that I can have his room and he will bunk in with a friend. So, all is well and I will be spared one more arduous day with my family.

Liam and I chatted happily all the way and by the time we get there we are the best of friends.

As soon as we reach Kingsley Manor my mouth drops open in awe. Wow! This place is gorgeous.

Liam has grown quiet and I smile at him reassuringly.

'Come on, let's do this. We'll make it fun; they won't know what's hit them.'

He smiles, but I can feel his anxiety. Gosh, what can be so bad about this? It certainly beats the weddings I've ever been to at the village hall.

As he retrieves the bags from the boot of the car and pays the taxi driver, I look around me with appreciation. There is a grand entrance flanked by two large potted trees, that are covered with fairy lights. A beautiful wreath sits proudly on a huge wooden door and the place screams wealth. Both Liam and I look a little scruffy if I'm honest after our journey, so I hope we don't meet anyone before I've had a chance to scrub up.

As we head inside across the polished tiled floor, I take in the opulence of the place.

A fire burns in the grate of a huge impressive fireplace, around which are placed several comfortable settees. Beautiful flower arrangements are strategically placed on large tables, which groan under the weight of them.

A long reception desk is at one end, which we head over to.

The receptionist smiles at us politely. 'Good afternoon. Welcome to Kingsley Manor. Are you booked to stay with us?'

Liam smiles and I watch as she falls under his spell. 'Yes, Mr. Goodwin and Miss.....'

I interrupt. 'Anderson.'

The receptionist looks down at a sheaf of papers and then pushes one across the desk.

'If you'll sign in, I will get your key.'

She is soon back and presents him with a huge key tied to a long red ribbon.

'You are in the Master's suite. Top floor, to the right of the lift. It's the last one at the end of the corridor. Will you be requiring a wake-up call in the morning?'

He shakes his head. 'No thank you, we'll be fine.'

Suddenly, we hear somebody bellow loudly, 'Liam! I thought that was you.'

As we turn, I see an older version of Liam heading towards us positively beaming. Closely followed by a regal-looking lady who is smiling happily.

Liam smiles and taking my hand pulls me close to his side.

'Dad, mum, it's great to see you. Let me introduce you to Annie, my girlfriend.'

I don't miss the surprise in his parent's eyes as they take in the messy, unruly sight of me. I have tangled hair and minimal makeup. My clothes are crumpled and I look completely out of place here. I register the flash of disapproval in his mother's eyes and my heart sinks.

She holds out her hand and says politely. 'I'm pleased to meet you.'

She turns to Liam and holds out her arms and he kisses her on both cheeks.

'Mum you look great.'

She sniffs. 'Flatterer. I'm sure I look anything but. This wedding has been exhausting already.'

His father appraises me, and somehow, I feel as if I don't quite measure up to their expectations. As if he senses it, Liam lifts my hand to his lips and stares into my eyes.

'Listen, mum, dad, we've had a long tiring journey and need to freshen up. How about we meet in the bar in an hour? We can catch up then.'

His parents nod politely and watch as Liam drags me behind him to the lift.

Once safely inside, he lets out a deep breath.

'Sorry about my parents. They aren't usually so cold. Mum had hoped that I'd marry my last girlfriend. She was everything they liked and were disappointed when I ended it.'

I look at him with interest. 'What happened?'

He pulls a face. 'She turned out to be a complete bitch. No personality and no morals either. I found out she'd been seeing some other guy when she was away on a shoot. Although she was beautiful, she had zero personality and after a while I got bored. It may be looks that first attract, but personality is the sticking factor.'

Before I can reply, we reach our floor and suddenly the enormity of what I've agreed to sinks in. I must be mad. I have met a sexy stranger on a train and agreed to spend the night with him. Oh, ok not in the same room, but what if he had other ideas all along? Suddenly, I feel a panic attack coming on and say weakly. 'Have you got any brandy left?'

Liam laughs softly. 'No, but I'll stock it up from the mini bar. Don't worry, you're safe with me, I promise.'

I follow him down the carpeted hallway, past several impressive wooden doors to the door at the end.

'The Master's Suite,' is emblazoned in gold lettering on the door and I watch with interest as Liam unlocks it with the huge key.

As he holds the door open, I walk into paradise!

Chapter Eight

'Liam, this place is amazing!'

He laughs and sets the bags down onto the floor. 'Yes, I wonder why we've been given such a great room?'

I nod. Great room indeed. It appears to be made up of a group of rooms, one of which is a small sitting area overlooking the beautiful grounds. I walk through a door into a massive bedroom where a fabulous four-poster bed dominates the centre. Flower arrangements are everywhere and the décor is modern and tasteful.

Excitedly, I open a door in the corner which leads into a modern bathroom with the largest shower I've ever seen. White fluffy towels hug the heated rail and two large comfy robes hang on the back of the door. Even the complimentary toiletries are Jo Malone. Wow! and Wow! I may not leave this room at all.

I walk back into the sitting area and watch as Liam pours us a couple of large brandies from a cut-glass decanter on the table.

He holds one out to me and grins. 'More Dutch courage for the troops.'

I take the glass and sink onto the sumptuous settee.

'This place is impressive. You can leave me here if you like.'

He laughs softly.

'Can't do that I'm afraid. A deal's a deal. You're going to keep me protected from the wildlife. I'll need you with me at all times if I'm to make it out alive.'

I snort and then cough to cover it up. How embarrassing! 'So, what's the plan?'

He sighs and sinks down next to me. 'We'll get changed and head off to meet the others. I'll take a few photographs of the happy couple and their guests, after which, we all sit down to an excruciating night with the family. Hopefully, we can make our escape quite early, citing exhaustion from the journey. We can come back here and watch a film or something and then you have the bed and I'll take this couch. You'll be perfectly safe because you can lock your door. Tomorrow after breakfast, I'll take some more photos and then we attend the ceremony. Hopefully, we'll be kept busy and not have to interact with the natives for too long. Then we can crash here again before heading off to phase two of our operation.'

I smile, once again bathed in a brandy glow. Gosh, I really should stop drinking this stuff. The AA initials that I have will take on a much more sinister meaning if I succumb to this heady, demon drink.

'Sounds good to me. Do you want the shower first, or can I?'

Liam smiles. 'You go. I'll just unpack and polish my lens.'

He winks, as I head off to bathroom paradise.

Soon, I'm ready and grateful that I packed my reliable little black dress. Despite the bad memories of the last time I wore it, it's all I have and I don't have any money for a new one given my sorry circumstances.

I went all out to make myself look as presentable as I can. Seeing Liam's parent's reactions to me earlier hit a nerve. I don't want anyone to wonder why on earth he is with me, after all, who likes that sort of humiliation.

So, I made a huge effort and am feeling quite proud of the result.

As I head into the little sitting room, Liam looks up and I watch as his face looks a little shocked if I'm honest. Just for a second, there is silence and then he jumps up and shakes his head.

'You look great, Annie. I can't believe it's really you.'

I roll my eyes. 'Oh, shut up, who did you think it was? I didn't look that bad before, did I?'

He laughs and then grins wickedly. 'Just give me 10 minutes and I'll be with you.'

He hurries off and I eye the brandy decanter longingly. Gosh, I'm turning into some sort of lush already and I've only been introduced to the drink for 5 minutes. I need some distraction therapy.

So, instead, I grab my phone and set about texting my mother.

Hi Mum

Change of plan. Something came up and I'll be a couple of days late. Expect me on Sunday instead and make up another bed because I'm bringing my new boyfriend.

Tell you all about it when I see you.

Love You

Anne x

There! The deed is done and there's no turning back now.

I hear Liam coming and my heart lurches. This is going to be interesting.

We stand silently in the lift as it propels us towards our stage. We are both quiet and I can tell that Liam is nervous.

I am silent for a whole other matter. Liam, as it turns out, is GORGEOUS!! When he came back into the room, I fought a huge battle with myself to just stop my mouth from falling open.

Freshly showered and smelling like an aftershave advert, he approached. He is wearing smart trousers and a white shirt that clings to him, showing off an amazing body that is straining to get out.

His hair is damp and begging for my hand to run through it.

I had to shake myself and picture him as Jason from the office because if I allow myself, I could very quickly become infatuated with this sexy stranger.

He in turn, is quiet and appears pre-occupied. I can feel my heart thumping and once again the thought of that brandy is playing heavily on my mind.

The lift comes to a stop and Liam smiles as he holds out his hand.

'Come on, girlfriend, let the games begin.'

As I take his hand, I feel like a shy girl on a first date. I really must get a grip.

We head into the bar and almost at once I hear the familiar bellow of his father. 'Over here son.'

We look around and I see his parents sitting with a group of people near the fireplace. It looks ultra-intimidating and I feel the nerves taking hold.

Liam squeezes my hand reassuringly and whispers. 'Don't worry, Annie, I won't leave you.'

I swallow hard and follow him into battle.

As we approach, I feel the interested stares of the waiting guests. Liam's mother smiles at me and waves around at her friends. 'Meet, Annie, Liam's new girlfriend.'

I smile around at the gathering and like his mum, I notice the surprise in their eyes as they take in the sight of me. Oh hell!

Liam nods to everyone and then his father shouts, 'Come and sit down and I'll pour you both a glass of champagne. Charlotte and Eric will be down shortly and then we can go in for dinner.'

Liam pulls me down next to him and his father hands us both a glass.

The lady to the other side of me leans in and says softly.

'Hi, I'm Kim. Listen, take no notice of this lot, you could be Kate Middleton and you wouldn't be worthy.'

I look at her in surprise. 'What do you mean?'

She laughs softly. 'Liam's ex is April Loveday, you know, the supermodel and face of Chanel. Well, Grace and Michael dined out on it at every opportunity. Their son, with the hottest girl on the planet. They were planning a huge society wedding that would cement their status among the elite. Then for some strange reason Liam ended it with no explanation. They are still getting over the shock so expect them to be a little frosty at first.'

I just stare at her in dismay. No wonder they look so disappointed. If they think I'm her replacement then I can understand it myself. My goodness, April Loveday is a goddess. There is no more beautiful woman that ever walked this earth. I know she cheated on him but even so…. He's obviously gone mad because nobody in their right mind would finish with April Loveday.

Kim laughs softly and squeezes my arm. 'Listen honey, I told you for your own good. Every one of these guests was hoping that the happy couple would reconcile and she would be in attendance.

Apparently, they booked him into the best room, other than the honeymoon suite, for that very reason. The fact that he's turned up with you is huge and I expect this will be a rocky couple of days for you. Liam will be ok, I mean, he just absorbs himself in his photography and is oblivious to everything. You, however, may not be so blind.

If it's any consolation, I hated April and cheered silently when he dumped her. I actually gained a lot of respect for Liam and wish you both well.'

She gets called over to talk to another lady and I sink back in my seat in shock. He could have warned me!!

Liam looks around and raises his eyes. 'Are you ok, Annie?'

I shake my head. 'I think I need your brandy on me at all times.'

He looks at me and then over to Kim and the realisation hits. 'She told you then?'

I nod.

He looks annoyed. 'I should have warned you I suppose, but I didn't think it mattered. If anyone knew the real reason why I dumped her, they would understand.'

I look at him intrigued. 'What because she cheated on you?'

He nods grimly. 'Anyway, take no notice of the gossip mongers. We're here to have fun and they can think all they want. There is no hope in hell that I would ever get back with her. She may be beautiful, but she is ugly inside. You are worth five hundred if not a thousand of her and don't let anyone tell you otherwise.'

I can feel the others watching us with curiosity, so I just smile at Liam and lean towards him. I can tell he's surprised and I whisper in his ear, 'It would appear we have an audience. I am about to become the best girlfriend you've ever had. By the end of this wedding, they will only have one name on their lips—mine! I hope you're ready for this.'

He laughs softly and his eyes twinkle. Squeezing my hand, he leans even closer and whispers, 'Bring it on, girlfriend. The trouble is—are you ready for me?'

Suddenly, we are interrupted by a loud cheer and we pull apart and see what must be the happy couple enter the bar.

Immediately, I feel Liam tense up and he looks over to the groom with a hard look. I follow his gaze and see an attractive couple standing before us, hand in hand.

His cousin is beautiful. She has long blonde hair and is wearing a pale blue trouser suit. Her jewellery looks amazing and I can tell it's the real deal. I look with interest at the groom. He seems ok, not at all like I imagined. He is holding tightly onto her hand and appears handsome and successful. His clothes look immaculate and he has a nice tan which makes him look healthy and relaxed. He is beaming around at everyone and if I'm honest, the picture is of the perfect couple.

Charlotte, says 'hi' to everyone and then squeals when she sees Liam.

'Liam, thank god you're here. I wasn't sure if you would actually come.'

I watch as his face softens, and he heads over and hugs her warmly.

'I wouldn't miss it for the world. You look beautiful by the way.'

She giggles adorably and then Liam turns to Eric. I watch in fascination as his eyes narrow and his expression hardens. It seems awkward and the two just nod at each other before Liam comes back to join me. I register the couple's surprise as Liam takes my hand and says, 'This is Annie, my girlfriend. Annie darling, meet my cousin Charlotte and her intended Eric.'

I smile at them warmly and Charlotte says in amazement.

'Gosh, Liam, you kept this quiet.'

She smiles warmly at me. 'It's good to meet you, Annie. I must say Liam has fallen on his feet with you, you're gorgeous.'

I can feel my cheeks flaming as I see the faces of the rest of them. They obviously don't agree with anything she just said.

Eric smiles politely. 'It's nice to meet you, Annie. I hope this isn't too much of an ordeal for you.'

I just smile happily at everyone. 'Thanks for having me. When Liam asked me to come and meet the family, I didn't really expect it to mean the entire clan. It's great to meet you all though.'

They all smile and then the conversation turns to the wedding. I listen as they all chatter about the guests, who's coming with who and whether it will rain tomorrow. Liam leans over and whispers. 'First hurdle over with. Just the meal and then we can get out of here, duty done.'

I smile at him, suddenly feeling very much the 'cuckoo in the nest.' These people are all well out of my league. They mix in a world I know nothing about. It's obvious from their clothes and their conversation. This weekend is going to be harder than I first thought because for once, I feel inferior in every way, and I don't like it one bit.

Chapter Nine

Liam is kept quite busy before dinner, taking photos of everyone. I watch him with interest as he sets about his work.

He is obviously a true professional because he snaps away, ordering the guests into all sorts of poses and appears totally absorbed by it all. I am really enjoying watching him.

Kim comes and stands next to me.

'I never introduced myself properly before. I'm Kim, Liam's Aunt, Graces' sister.'

I smile. 'It's good to meet you, Kim.'

She grins. 'I'm glad he's dating somebody normal at last. The trouble is, he is surrounded by so much perfection every day, it clouds his judgement on what really matters.'

I look at her in surprise. 'Why? I mean, I know he's a photographer, but surely he's a good judge of character?'

She laughs. 'Well, you're very understanding, I'll say that for you. Any other girl would hate the fact their boyfriend spends all day and sometimes nights photographing the top models in the world for

British Vogue. I'm not sure I could hack it, especially looking like he does; it's a powerful combination. These girls' lust after their photographers, especially when he's as drop dead gorgeous as Liam. When April became his girlfriend, they all backed off. After all, who could compete with her? However, now that's changed…. Well, don't expect an easy ride, that's all I'm saying.'

She laughs as she sees my expression. 'Come on, I'll get you a drink and you can tell me all about yourself and how you met. I'm bored with wedding conversation, anyway.'

She guides me over to the bar and suddenly, the need to get absolutely wasted is high on my list of priorities. It's just a good thing this is all fake, imagine if I really was his girlfriend.

Kim turns out to be great fun. She gives me the lowdown on all the guests and the stories about them have me in stitches. I discover she runs a PR company not far from where I used to work. When I told her what happened she looked annoyed. She asked for my business card and said she would be in touch after Christmas and would see what she could do to help.

It appears that I'm becoming a super networker. Surely one of these chance meetings will materialise into an actual job offer?

Soon Liam comes to find me, and I note the weariness in his eyes. 'Hey, Annie, sorry I left you.'

Kim laughs. 'So you should be. I've filled Annie in on every gruesome detail about you, and if she's still here in the morning I obviously failed miserably in putting her off.'

Liam grins as she walks away. 'I see my Aunt is her usual self.'

I laugh. 'She's great. In fact, she's the only one who has spoken to me at all. I never knew you were so sought after though.'

He pulls a face. 'Drawback of the job. I sometimes wish I had taken up a different type of photography. I'm sure animals and landscapes are a lot more fun to work with.'

I laugh. 'So how long have you worked for Vogue?'

He shrugs. 'Two years. It sounds more glamorous than it is. Most of the time it's just waiting around endlessly for hair and make-up, not to mention the tantrums of some of the models and designers.'

I grin. 'I'm sure you throw your own fair share of tantrums.'

He laughs and then we hear them calling us into dinner.

'Come on. Let's eat and then I'll get you out of this hellish place.'

As I take his hand, I suddenly realise that I'm extremely hungry.

We are sat between his parents and his Aunt Kim. She is on her own and I wonder what her story is.

Halfway through the meal, I find out that her husband died suddenly of a heart attack. He left her very comfortably off with a company to run. She relished the challenge, and it now dominates her life.

Liam's parents meanwhile totally ignore me which suits me fine. They chat away to him, asking him all about his work and name dropping at every opportunity.

I also take the chance to study the happy couple. I don't know why Liam is so against Eric? He appears handsome and charming and is extremely attentive to Charlotte. She is positively glowing and they appear very much in love.

By the end of the meal I am ready for my bed. The large amount of food I ate is battling with the alcohol in my system and what with our long journey I am now done in.

Liam notices my drooping eyelids and looks around at the rest of the table. 'If you'll excuse us, I need to get Annie off to bed.'

I don't miss the smirks on everyone's faces and just smile at Liam sexily as he pulls me from my seat and we hurry out of the room.

As we head upstairs, he grins at me apologetically. 'I'm sorry, Annie. You must be wondering what you've agreed to here. At least we get the worst over first; I mean, your family will be a doddle after this lot.'

I don't answer and my heart lurches at his words. Oh my god, he has absolutely no idea what he's let himself in for. His family will seem normal when faced with mine. I'm not sure whether to warn him or not.

We reach our room and he flops down onto the couch.

'Finally, we can relax. Do you fancy a film, or just want to crash?'

I sink down next to him heavily. 'A film would be good, anything but a wedding one though. In fact, it may be best to watch a good old-fashioned one about death, destruction and blowing people up to get us in the mood for tomorrow.'

He grins. 'Terminator it is then.'

As he pours us both a Brandy, I kick off my shoes and make myself comfortable.

Chapter Ten

The sound of the telephone ringing invades my dreams. That had better not be Tosser again!

Strangely, I feel disorientated and appear to ache all over. Any movement brings with it a sudden pain and I open one eye to test the water.

It appears that I'm tangled up in a body that is somehow connected to mine.

Suddenly, a hazy memory of the alcohol infested night before swims into my consciousness and I groan.

Then I hear a muffled voice growling. 'Someone shut that blasted phone up before my head explodes.'

I try to sit up and in doing so dislodge the arm of my captor.

I groan and my eyes focus on the aftermath of the night before.

Liam and I are still on the couch wearing our now crumpled clothes from the night before. I'm not sure how many films we watched, but it would appear the decanter is now empty.

Liam pulls himself up and rubs his eyes and I'm instantly annoyed at how gorgeous he still looks. All rough and sexy with designer stubble and ruffled hair. Me, on the other hand, I must look like the lush I'm fast turning into.

He grabs the ringing phone angrily and barks, 'What?!!'

I can hear some sort of high-pitched voice talking quickly on the other end. Liam just grunts and runs his fingers through his hair distractedly.

Then he says shortly. 'Yeah, we'll be there in 20 minutes.'

As he puts the phone down, he looks at me and grins ruefully.

'Sorry, duty calls. They want some pre-wedding shots of the happy couple and guests.'

I groan. 'Well tell them it's bad luck for the groom to see the bride before the service. What's happened to the traditions these days?'

Liam grins. 'Not much tradition left. I mean, the bride and groom appear to be already sharing the marital bed and have been for some time. The wedding is far from being conducted in a church and is part of an elaborate staged ceremony in what was once somebody's home.'

I grin. 'Point taken. Anyway, how the hell did we let this happen? Why on God's earth did I crash on this couch, when a five-star bed was waiting through those double doors?'

He laughs. 'Don't you remember anything about last night?'

Suddenly, I feel worried. 'Why, what did I do? Or should I say we?'

He laughs. 'Well, after we watched every Terminator film and drank all the brandy, we started talking about random things. One thing you divulged was a fascination with massage. You then proceeded to massage my feet while telling me every detail of what you hate about Tosser.'

I can feel my face burning. 'You're kidding, I hope.'

He laughs and pulls me up. 'No, but I can't remember the last time I had so much fun. I think you passed out around 3am and I sort of just followed you. I tried to wake you up, but you punched me and swore that you had a rape alarm and weren't afraid to use it.'

Now I am more mortified than I have ever been in my life—and that's saying something.

I shake my head. 'I'm sorry, Liam. You must wonder what the hell you've got yourself into with me.'

He laughs. 'Like I said, I enjoyed every minute. Now we've got precisely ten minutes to scrub up and meet the happy couple. Then begins the laborious task of capturing their happy day on film.'

I groan. 'Can't I stay here? They won't want me in any of them and I could test out the bed while I wait.'

He picks me up and throws me over his shoulder.

'You're not getting away with leaving me for the vultures. In you go woman and make yourself presentable. You are staying with me all day. A deal's a deal after all.'

Rather than struggle, I just take the opportunity to grab two seconds more sleep. Then he deposits me unceremoniously in the bathroom before leaving me to freshen up.

Freshen up? More like a complete overhaul. Panda eyes are so unattractive, not to mention black circles under them and tangled hair. Ten minutes to work a miracle—I think not!

Half an hour later we once again head downstairs. Somehow, I have managed to look semi-presentable and glare at Liam who appears to bear no scars from the night before.

He laughs as I frown at him. 'What's got you so angry?'

I huff. 'You and your ability to look as if you had 12 hours sleep followed by a spa. Meanwhile, I look like one of the Witches of Eastwick and have aged ten years in one night. If you so much as hint at getting me a brandy anytime soon, I'll call the Police and report you for dealing in hard drugs.'

He laughs and then tickles me relentlessly until I gasp for air.

It's this sight that greets his parents as they observe us when the lift doors open.

I don't miss the icy glare in his mother's eyes as she looks at her watch and sniffs.

'About time. We were just coming to find you. Please remember you have a duty to carry out and stop treating this as just an excuse for a dirty weekend.'

I almost can't look at Liam and try to look remorseful. Liam just shrugs and pulls me behind him as we go in search of the happy couple.

The wedding breakfast is amazing. The hotel has pulled out all the stops and there is every known breakfast item on the planet in the room.

The fellow guests are standing around, talking and sipping glasses of Buck's Fizz made with real champagne. Not the usual pre-made stuff that we buy from Tesco's either.

I grab a water instead. No alcohol for me today. Last night has taught me that it's not my friend.

Liam starts snapping away and I enjoy watching him work. The bride and groom look completely happy and in love. I am starting to wonder if Liam is a good judge of character because Eric appears a model boyfriend/ husband to be.

Liam's parents appear to be enjoying themselves chatting to the other guests and I just tuck myself away in the corner and sneak a croissant to help soak up the alcohol. This is where Kim finds me.

She laughs as she approaches and raises her eyes. 'Good night, darling?'

I shudder. 'I think so. I can't actually remember if I'm honest.'

She grins. 'Oh, to be young again.'

She stands next to me and looks around the room. 'Hopefully, we can ditch this charade and start eating soon. I'm famished and need to start getting ready early. I'm booked into the hotel hair salon in thirty minutes.'

I look interested. 'Wow, their own salon. I could so use a professional hairdresser right now.'

Kim laughs. 'Then come with me. The amount we're all paying I'm sure they'll be able to fit you in. I'm going with Grace and Lucy, the Bride's mother. One more won't hurt.'

I look at her with horror. The thought of being in a confined space with Grace is terrifying.

'Oh, it's ok. Liam won't let me out of his sight it seems, so I'll just trust in my own skills and put it up or something.'

Kim looks annoyed. 'One word of advice, Annie. Don't let a man control you. If they think they have you just where they want you, they lose interest.

Keep him guessing and don't succumb to his every wish.'

I almost want to laugh. If only she knew.

We are soon called to eat and I almost fall on the delicious pastries with my mouth open, ready to consume the delights that are attractively laid out in rustic, artisan style, baskets.

Liam joins me and piles his plate high with almost everything. Once again, I note his mother's disapproval.

We sit at a large table and tuck in. I need as much food as possible to soak up that brandy.

After my full cooked breakfast, cereal, croissant, Danish pastry and toast and Jam, I notice that most of the other women have only eaten a bowl of fruit salad and some muesli.
Once again, I see their looks of astonishment, as I crumple up my napkin and sink back in my chair.

Liam joins me and we sit like two beached, basking, whales after a blowout.

Liam smiles at me and winks. 'Thank god you actually eat, Annie. There's nothing worse than eating with someone who just sniffs at a piece of grapefruit, while downing more water than the human body can stand. It's quite lonely eating on your own.'

I laugh softly. 'Well, it must take quite a lot of work and effort to be so perfect. I should really take some lessons you know.'

Liam frowns and looks at me with those piercing blue eyes.

'You are perfect the way you are and don't let anyone tell you differently. At least you have a great personality and know how to have a good time. Life with you is certainly entertaining.'

I smile but inside his words sting. Yes, that's me, good old Annie. The reliable, good for a laugh girl, that's everybody's friend and nobody's desire. Even my supposed boyfriend forgot about me when I was out of sight. And as for being entertaining—he may not think so after he's met my family. I have a feeling his opinion will change quite drastically then.

Once breakfast is out of the way we all head outside to the grounds. Once again, we must endure near arctic temperatures while Liam takes photos with frozen berries and tastefully decorated Christmas trees.

I am not required in any of the photographs which suits me fine. Instead, I jump up and down on the spot to keep from getting frostbite.

Then we all head back inside for warming hot chocolates and to thaw out by the fire.

After more polite chatter we all head off to primp and preen ourselves into the glamorous guests that this wedding demands.

Chapter Eleven

As I look at myself in the mirror, I'm quite pleased with my reflection. My Christmas dress looks good enough to pass any wedding guest test. It is appropriately red and hugs my curves in all the right places.

I have made up my face as professionally as I can and curled my hair so that it hangs down my back with some bounce and volume. Finally, I feel more like myself and can try to forget the lush that I have appeared to have turned into since yesterday.

I head outside to the sitting room to look for Liam. He is sitting on the settee sorting his camera out and he looks up as I approach.

He appears quite astonished if I'm honest and seems lost for words. After a minute, he shakes his head and smiles.

'You look amazing, Annie. That colour really suits you.'

I laugh happily. 'Flattery will get you everywhere, boyfriend. You don't look so bad yourself.'

My words don't convey just what a hot dish this guy really is. He has scrubbed up better than I ever thought he could. His suit looks well cut and expensive and his freshly showered hair is just begging for my attention. I can't believe how much better he gets every time I see him and I swallow hard as I inwardly pant at the sight of him. Wow! If only he really was my boyfriend.

He grins ruefully. 'Well, let the ordeal commence. Please accept my apologies in advance for the gruelling nightmare that is about to unfold.'

I laugh. 'Believe me. Nothing that happens today will prepare you for the days ahead. Just enjoy a little bit of normal for as long as you can, because what lies in store for you will make this all seem very tame in comparison.'

He looks at me questioningly. 'Then I will look forward to seeing what you have in store for me.'

He holds out his arm and winks.

'Come on, my gorgeous girl. Let's show them what we've got.'

We head downstairs and into the bar area. I see that our numbers have grown as more wedding guests have arrived; all looking amazing in their wedding finery.

Liam grabs two glasses of champagne from the tray of a passing waiter and offers one to me.

'Here, drink up, Annie. This will help get you through.'

I roll my eyes. 'Are you trying to get me drunk again?'

He laughs and then we hear a loud voice shout,

'Liam, you scoundrel. I've been looking for you everywhere.'

Swinging around, we see a large group of guys, with what appears to be their girlfriends in attendance. They look about our age - early twenties and it would appear they are Liam's friends.

He laughs and pulls me over to join them. 'Hi Tom, everyone. Meet Annie, my girlfriend.'

I smile nervously and once again note the surprise in their eyes. The girls look astonished and the guys grin and look me up and down. Tom smiles and holds out his hand.

'Charmed to meet you, Annie. My god, Liam, you don't hang around. How do you manage to grab such gorgeous girls being the complete nerd that you are?'

Liam laughs, while the girls roll their eyes. Obviously wishful thinking on Tom's part because Liam is no nerd, given the reaction of the girls in the group.

One of them smiles at me and far from judging me she appears warm and friendly.

'Hi Annie, I'm Cindy and this is Ellen, Jenny and Melissa. For our sins, these are our guys. We've been trying to ditch them for years, but they just won't take the hint.'

One of the guys laughs and puts his arm around her shoulders.

'Take no notice of her, Annie. These girls know they're onto a good thing and that's us. Why do you think they stick around? They know they wouldn't find anyone better than us if they spent the rest of their lives looking.'

The others laugh and I finally relax. At last, some people who seem like good fun and don't appear to judge me.

The guys all start talking about sport and the girls draw me into their group. Melissa smiles and nods towards Liam.

'Lucky you, Annie. You've met a great guy in Liam. We're glad he's found someone nice. I must say, you're just what he needed after what he went through with that bitch April.'

The others nod in agreement.

I look interested. 'How long were they together for?'

Melissa looks thoughtful. 'I think it was about six months. At first, they were the golden couple. The media loved them and Liam seemed happy. The trouble is, she's high maintenance and didn't ever really fit in with the group. After a while they drifted away from us and we saw less of them. The last we knew; Liam had ended it and wouldn't say why. Word is, she cheated on him and he is unable to forgive such a betrayal. Despite everything, he's a loyal soul and doesn't give his heart away lightly.'

Jenny nods. 'I heard she regrets it enormously. Apparently, she wants him back and will stop at nothing. Despite the fact he is so gorgeous, he is also the best photographer around. He can make anyone look a million dollars and she needs him to make her look good in every sense of the word. Watch out Annie, if April Loveday wants something, she usually gets it.'

I just shrug and smile. 'It's fine. I trust Liam and if he wanted to get back with her, then it wasn't meant to be. I'm not going to let it affect me.'

I register the admiration in the girl's eyes. They obviously think I'm some sort of super-cool girl. If Liam really was my guy, I would be a seething mass of anxiety after hearing that. There wouldn't be a brandy bottle safe in this whole hotel if it really was the case.

I notice Liam on his phone and his eyes meet mine, shrouded in exasperation.

Coming over he looks annoyed. 'Sorry, Annie, duty calls. I'm needed to photograph the bridal party. We can catch up with these guys later.'

Cindy interrupts. 'Leave Annie with us, Liam. The last thing she wants is to follow you around.'

Liam shakes his head. 'Sorry, she is coming with me. I don't want her out of my sight for a second, especially with you lot telling her stories about me.'

I smile and follow him, noticing their incredulous expressions. Oh well, a deal is a deal, after all.

Chapter Twelve

I follow Liam to the bridal suite. If I thought our room was nice this is Buckingham Palace in comparison.

It's like a small apartment and the interior is worthy of inclusion in the smartest of Interiors magazines. The windows are draped in ivory silk and the cream carpet is so deep it could swallow you up like quicksand. Tasteful furniture is placed at intervals around the room, holding beautiful flower arrangements that fill the air with their intoxicating scent.

Mirrors line the walls making everything seem even bigger and there are beautiful paintings on neutral paintwork. My goodness, how the other half live.

The room is filled with beautiful girls, obviously Charlotte's bridesmaids. They are dressed in a deep red satin and have little white fur bolero jackets slung around their shoulders. There is great excitement in the room and the noise is tremendous.

As they see Liam the excitement in the air increases. They openly gaze at him in adoration, which turns to astonishment when they notice me. This is not turning out to be a great trip down the road of self-esteem for me. I never thought I was that bad, but the way these people have all looked at me this weekend, I feel like Fiona from Shrek.

Our attention shifts as the double doors open and Grace enters the room with the bride's mother. Lucy is wiping a tear from her eye and then I see why.

Walking behind her and looking like Cinderella, is Charlotte.

We all gasp in admiration because a more beautiful bride I have never seen.

She looks stunning. Her dress is pure white silk. It hugs her body all the way to her waist and then falls around her in a cascade of ruffles and silk. Her hair is piled on top of her head and her blue eyes sparkle with beauty and excitement. Her jewellery vies with the rest of her to command attention and a long veil sits perched on her head, framing the beauty that wears it with so much style.

I watch Liam as he gazes at Charlotte in disbelief.

Crossing over to her, he kisses her cheek and whispers something in her ear.

She blushes and looks at him, her eyes shining brightly.

I almost want to cry myself. She looks amazing and I hope with all my heart that Liam is wrong about Eric. Nobody should hurt this beautiful creature before us. She is a Disney princess and should be forever adored.

I blend into the background as Liam sets to work.

He takes many photographs of Charlotte and the women in the room. The whole atmosphere is of happiness and excitement and it's catching. I feel happy to be a small part of this magical moment. Witnessing the love that Charlotte and her mother share takes my breath away.

Her friends appear a good bunch and there is lots of laughter. Liam captures it all and I can only imagine how amazing those photographs are going to be.

Nobody notices I am here. I am not part of this scene and have no business being here. I understand that and it doesn't matter. I just hope that one day this will be in my future. How I envy Charlotte at this moment.

Suddenly, there is a knock at the door and Grace opens it, revealing Charlotte's father waiting outside.

As soon as he sees his daughter tears come to his eyes and he looks at her with such an expression of love, that I don't even bother to stop the tears from running down my face.

He is the proudest man on the planet at this moment in time. This is a beautiful moment that will stay with me forever.

Liam snaps away and there is a hush in the room.

Then Grace starts ordering everyone out.

'Come on everyone, places, places. We need to get going, the wedding will be starting soon.'

The bridesmaids start rushing around gathering their things and the room soon starts to empty.

I feel a little awkward as I don't know what to do. Grace sees me and I don't miss the irritation in her voice as she says, 'Oh, Annie, you need to get to the ceremony. Follow me and I'll find you a place to sit.'

Liam looks up sharply. 'She can follow me, I need her with me.'

His mother's eyes flash and she retorts, 'She'll follow me and you will carry on with your job. You'll have all the time in the world later on to be together.'

She pulls me from the room before he can answer and I flash him an apologetic smile as we go.

As I walk behind her, I feel the cold vibes emanating from her. We get to the lift and she looks at me and raises her eyes.

'I'm sorry to be so harsh, Annie. You must understand this wedding has been in the planning for a long time now. We are used to seeing Liam with April and it has come as quite a shock to everyone. Then he turns up with you and we don't have a minute to adjust to the situation.'

I smile apologetically. 'I'm sorry, Mrs. Goodwin. I can see how rude we've been. Please accept my apologies, I would never have come if I had thought it would make things difficult.'

Just for a moment her expression softens. 'No, I'm sorry, Annie. You seem like a lovely girl and none of this is your fault. In different circumstances, I would have very much enjoyed meeting you. The trouble is, Liam is such as secretive soul. He hides his emotions and feelings from us all and we know that the breakup affected him deeply. I was just worried that you were a re-bound from April. I would hate to think that he was using you to displace her from his heart. Just a word of advice, don't hold out too much hope for a future with Liam. He moves in powerful circles and you may struggle to keep up. His world is very different from the rest of ours and he needs to be with people like him. Enjoy the moment dear because that is all it will turn out to be.'

The lift comes and we travel downstairs in silence. I am really annoyed and a little hurt at her words. In other words, I am no good for Liam and he is using me until someone better comes along. Well thank goodness that really is the case, because if I really had been Liam's girlfriend, that woman would have destroyed me in seconds.

Now where is that brandy?

Chapter Thirteen

Grace pushes me into a seat at the back of the room and then heads off to the front. I look around me in awe at the amazing scene before me.

The room has been styled like a scene from a film.

We sit on silk-covered chairs with huge red satin bows fastened behind them. Candles are everywhere and burn brightly in the subdued lighting. Soft romantic music fills the air and the flower arrangements rise in splendour on every available surface.

The colour scheme is red and white with lots of glitter and silver. This is the most beautiful Christmas wedding that I have ever been to. It's magical and takes my breath away. Fairy lights twinkle like stars on the ceiling and cream roses merge with deep red poinsettias and crimson roses.

All around me sit the elite. The clothes and jewellery on the women must add up to a small fortune. The men look stylish and smart and I feel very much out of place.

I look at the groom and it strikes me how handsome he looks in his black tuxedo with matching red cummerbund.

He looks excited and happy and is laughing and joking with what appears to be his best man beside him.

Then the music starts and fills the room. There is a breathless anticipation as the doors open and the groom takes his place at the front before the registrar.

I notice Liam making his way down the side of the room to the front and he catches my eye and smiles. Just for a second my heart flutters. I must be more affected by this wedding than I thought because at this moment in time, I really wish I was his girlfriend more than anything I have ever wanted in my life before.

Then we are told to stand, and the fanfare begins.

All eyes turn to the back of the room as the bridal party makes its way inside.

Two gorgeous little flower girls, dressed in white princess dresses, carry little baskets containing rose petals. They scatter handfuls of petals before them to cries of *aah* and *how sweet*.

Then come the grown-up bridesmaids. All looking beautiful and smiling around them in excitement.

Then there's an audible gasp as Charlotte comes into view. A vision of elegance and poise and looking like an Angel.

Tears fill my eyes as I see the proud look on her father's face. He stands rigid and proud, guiding his precious cargo to the waiting arms of another. His little girl no longer, all grown up and fleeing the nest.

My heart swells as I see the emotion in his face. Charlotte gazes around her like a startled fawn. Her lip trembles and her eyes are bright with unshed tears. She grips her father's arm like a lifeline as she stares ahead of her at the man who has captured her heart and is her ultimate destiny.

I can't believe how moved I am by the whole spectacle. I can't look away as I watch the scene unfold. This is a beautiful moment that I will cherish forever. The lady beside me gasps as they pass.

'Oh, my goodness, she is so beautiful.'

I must agree. Move aside April Loveday, there's a new supermodel in town. There is not a woman on earth that can outshine this bride in her moment of glory.

I watch as Eric's face reflects the emotions inside him. He gazes at his bride with sheer disbelief. His eyes are ablaze with love for her and I watch him battle with his emotions as she approaches. This man would lay down his life for the woman before him at this moment in time. My heart swells as I witness the love between these two people. Liam is wrong about Eric; I just know in my heart he is.

Soon, I am swept away by the pure romance of the ceremony. The music is soulful and the vows moving. There is not a dry eye in the room as the bride and groom declare their devotion before their witnesses.

All too soon it is over and they are declared man and wife. Cheering breaks out and the music peals out, declaring the happy moment for all to see.

As they walk down the aisle as man and wife, the woman beside me whispers, 'I give it two years, tops.'

Once the bridal party is safely outside having their photographs taken, I join the long line of people vacating the room. I hear somebody calling my name and see Melissa waving me over.

'Hey, Annie, over here.'

I head over towards them gratefully and she grins. 'Sorry. I had saved you a seat but didn't notice you until it was too late. Here grab a drink and relax. The worst is over and now we can eat, drink and be merry.'

I smile at her happily. 'That was such a lovely ceremony. I don't think I've ever seen such a beautiful couple. They obviously love each other very much.'

Cindy snorts. 'Well, appearances can be deceptive.'

I look at her in astonishment. 'What do you mean?'

Melissa throws her a warning look and then smiles thinly.

'Let's just say, Charlotte absolutely adores Eric and has realised her dream come true today. Eric, on the other hand, has got what he wanted most, a trophy wife who turns the occasional blind eye. Don't be fooled by this fairy-tale wedding, Annie, this was a business transaction that both have walked into, very much with their eyes open.'

Before I can comment, I feel a hand slip into mine and I look up into Liam's incredibly sexy eyes.

'Hey gorgeous, I missed you.'

I smile at him and flutter my eyelashes - for appearances only of course.

'Hey, boyfriend, are you now officially free to party?'

He rolls his eyes. 'I wish. Just a few more shots and I should be. How about you, are these guys looking after you ok?'

I smile happily. 'Yes, of course, I'm fine. Don't worry about me, it's all getting interesting.'

The girls look at Liam innocently as he frowns.

'I don't think I want to know. Anyway, is there any alcohol around here? I need something to get me through the meal ordeal ahead.'

I laugh and grab him a glass of champagne from a nearby tray.

'Here you go, it's not brandy but it will have to do.'

He grins and looks at the others. 'If Annie even hints that she wants a brandy, move away. This girl is not to be trusted around that particular drink.'

I laugh at their shocked expressions and roll my eyes.

'Don't believe a word of it ladies. If it wasn't for Liam, I wouldn't have ever touched a drop. He forced it on me to get me to agree to be his girlfriend. He's now worried that once I am out of the influence, I will sober up long enough to realise what a mess I have got myself into.'

He laughs along with the others and Melissa grins.

'Sounds like a match made in Heaven. You appear very well suited.'

One of Liam's friends comes over and grins wickedly at him.

'Hey, Liam. I just heard that Victoria Craven is coming tonight. You'll need a few more of those before she arrives if I'm not mistaken.'

They all laugh as Liam pulls a face.

'Ugh. I just hope you've all got my back, otherwise Annie and I are leaving right now.'

His friend laughs and Melissa turns to the guy.

'Where did you hear that? I thought she fell out with Charlotte months ago.'

He grins. 'It would appear they made up. Anyway darling, are you going to escort me to the line-up? I believe it's feeding time at the Zoo.'

Melissa rolls her eyes and takes his arm.

'Come on then, Mark. Just keep your hands off my food and other items close to my heart and we'll be fine.'

He laughs and kisses her neck.

'Can't promise to keep my hands of you, Mel, you're just too tempting.'

Liam rolls his eyes at me and takes my hand. 'Come on, Annie, breakfast seems like ages ago. You up for another feast?'

I grin. 'Wouldn't miss it for the world.'

Chapter Fourteen

Ok, I am now officially stuffed. The meal was amazing, like everything else at this wedding. I sat with Liam and his friends and had a really good time. They are all great fun and for the first time since coming here I relaxed.

I enjoyed watching Liam with his friends. It's obvious they all have a strong bond, and they kept me in stitches throughout the meal.

Even the speeches were good. Once again, I had tears in my eyes as I heard them. They must all be wrong because the love that Eric and Charlotte have for each other was plain for everyone to see. Nobody could fake true love - surely? I vow to ask Liam why he hates Eric. It must be something bad because Liam appears to like nearly everyone else here.

Soon it's time to head outside while they get ready for the evening party. Liam's mother stops by our table and frowns at him.

'You're needed again, Liam. I'm sure Annie will be fine with your friends while you take some more photos.'

Liam smiles ruefully and turns to me and whispers.

'She's probably right. You would be better off with the guys. I won't be long though, I promise.'

I just smile at him reassuringly. 'Look I'll be fine. You go and do what you have to. I'll catch you later.'

He leans over and whispers. 'Thanks, Annie. I mean it, for everything. Having you here is making this all a lot more bearable. Has anyone ever told you, you make the hottest girlfriend?'

I smile at him sexily. 'How much have you had to drink already, Liam? You've obviously had more than I thought.'

To my surprise, he just kisses me on the cheek and whispers. 'I mean every word.'

Then he follows his mother, leaving me feeling a little thrown if I'm honest. There was a sincerity to his look that didn't fit with the gentle teasing that we usually do. Why does my heart now beat a little faster and my brain buzz with excitement? What is happening to me?

Feeling a little wrong-footed I look at Cindy who is next to me and stutter. 'I'm just heading to the ladies. Will you be here, or are you moving outside?'

She looks at the others. 'If we're not here then meet us in the bar. You know, the one we met at earlier. We'll grab you a drink if you like. They may be a while setting up, so we may as well make ourselves comfortable.'

I smile. 'Thanks, I won't be long.'

I make my way to the ladies and take a moment to collect my thoughts. For the first time since I met Liam, I am thinking about what I agreed to. I must have been mad to head off with a stranger that I just met to a wedding of strangers. The fact they nearly all hate me was unexpected and I can't say I'm enjoying that part of it.

I am enjoying Liam's company though. He is great fun and mild-mannered. We have fallen into an easy relationship as friends, which is why I shouldn't read any more into it. He has just split from a supermodel and I am keeping the wannabees away. Then why do I suddenly want more?

This wedding has well and truly messed with my head. Thank goodness there's just tonight and then we can get the hell out of here. At least I'll never have to face his mother again!

As I sit on my porcelain throne pondering my situation, I hear voices outside the cubicle.

'Have you seen Liam's new girlfriend? Gosh, talk about lowering your standards.'

Someone giggles. 'Well, April is a huge act to follow. It's doubtful there's a girl on the planet who could fill her shoes.'

'I'd like to give it a try though.' Her friend laughs.

'Shame he's turned up with her replacement so soon. I wonder if she thinks he'll stay with her past this weekend?' *More laughter.*

'If she does, she's going to get a shock. From the look of her she should be counting her lucky stars that she's made it this far. I mean, I guess she's ok looking, but well out of Liam's league.'

Ok, that's it. I've had enough. How dare they talk about me as if I'm a second-class citizen and second best to some beautiful, rich, successful supermodel? I'm an Accountant for Gods' sake - enough said!

I explode from my solitude like a bullet from a gun and note with satisfaction their surprised and slightly worried expressions.

Fixing them both with my most deadly look, I snarl angrily.

'Just for the record, ladies, Liam is with me purely for the sex. As it happens, I provide him with everything that April couldn't. Appearance doesn't matter when you're blindfolded, gagged and tied up face down on the bed. You see, it takes a special kind of woman to please a man like Liam and I am happy to report I'm very much up to the job. Now, if you'll excuse me, I'd better be getting back before he spanks me stupid for taking too long. Enjoy your night, ladies and your boring sex lives because I am living the dream.'

I flick my hair back in pure diva style and then come face to face with the horrified faces of Liam's mum and Aunt Kim.

Oh, double Hell!!

There is silence as we all just look at each other in shock. I hear the giggles behind me and want to disappear into a pool of water. Kim's mouth twitches, and she says softly.

'There you are, Annie. Liam's looking for you. Off you go, we'll catch up later.'

I smile at her thankfully and nod to Liam's mum, who just stares at me with a stony expression.

Quickly, I edge past them and almost run out of the room.

Me and my big mouth. Now I've ruined everything.

I decide not to return to the wedding. This is all too much and I need to get away. So instead, I do what every coward does when faced with the enemy, I retreat and head off as quickly as I can to our room.

It's only when I'm face down on the bed—fully clothed I might add—that the floodgates open. Suddenly, I'm crying and can't appear to stop.

Finally, it has all caught up with me and I let it all out. The job, Gary, and now the abuse I have received since coming here. I am now officially a complete wreck and that is exactly as Liam finds me.

Suddenly, I find myself being pulled towards a hard, comforting, chest. He strokes my hair and kisses me on the top of my head.

'It's ok, Annie, let it all out.'

I sob uncontrollably in Liam's arms and I can't stop. Liam, as it turns out, is a true hero.

He pulls me back against the headboard and just holds me while I let it all out. No words are spoken, just one friend comforting another.

It must be a good ten minutes later that the sobs subside. As he hands me a tissue, he smiles and raises his eyes.

'So, beautiful, are you going to tell me what's wrong?'

I sniff and blow my nose loudly into the tissue. 'Sorry, Liam. It's just all caught up with me. I heard some girls talking about me in the ladies and it made me see red. I'm afraid I said some awful things and then your mum and Aunt came in and heard them. Now they hate me even more, because they think I'm a sexed crazed hooker, who has corrupted their son and nephew. I now officially want to die and to never see any of them, ever again. The fact that I must go home to the mad house tomorrow is sending me over the edge. Not to mention that I'm jobless, loveless and soon to be homeless. I think that's all for now.'

Liam looks at me incredulously and then laughs. 'What did you say to them?'

I grin and look at him shamefaced. 'That we were into all sorts of kinky sex and that's the reason you went out with me.'

I have to laugh at the shock on his face before I cry again.

Suddenly, he grins and then laughs with me. 'I would have paid to see my mother's face, not to mention the rest of them. You obviously read more of that Fifty Shades book than I thought on the train.'

I laugh, sheepishly. 'It was the first thing that came into my head. So, you see I had to come up here. I must never be seen in decent company again.'

Liam pulls me up from the bed. 'You're joking aren't you. I wouldn't miss this for the world. I know, let's really get them talking.'

I look at him in surprise. 'Why, what do you have in mind?'

He grins. 'Ever had a Chinese burn, Annie?'

I laugh. 'I see where you're going with this. Do you worst, Master!'

He grins wickedly and I hold out my arms. He grabs hold of one of them and twists my wrist until I cry out. I study the red mark that has appeared proudly.

'Good job, now the other one.'

He does the other one and we laugh as we see the red marks on my wrists.

He then reaches up and ruffles my hair a bit more. 'There you go, nice and ravished. Let's go down and reap the rewards of our deception. It's time I enjoyed myself at this wedding.'

Giggling, I follow him from the room. What a great guy!

Chapter Fifteen

I admire my reflection in the mirror as we travel down in the lift. Liam is grinning at me and I meet his eyes in the reflection.

'Are you sure about this, Liam? I mean, I could just tell them the truth. Nobody would think badly of you then. You could say we are just friends and your mother would be happy and leave you alone. Why are you causing problems for yourself?'

Just for a moment his eyes darken and he looks angry. There's my angry man.

He shrugs. 'Because they need teaching a lesson. When I went out with April, I saw a side to my mother that I didn't like. She became a total bitch, only concerned with appearance and status. She revelled in my relationship and became popular amongst her crowd of loser friends. She dined out on her newfound popularity and saw a life she had only ever dreamed of. The fact that I was unhappy didn't matter. The only thing she cared about was that I was dating the most beautiful girl on the planet. What she didn't see was how ugly she was inside.'

I look interested and smile at him as I take his hand.

'What happened, Liam? What did she do to make you hate her so much?'

Before he can reply the lift stops and the door opens. He squeezes my hand.

'I'll tell you later. But now we must get this party started. No more photography for me, I am officially off duty and partying with my gorgeous girlfriend. You are gorgeous by the way; I'm not just saying that either. You have what April severely lacks - a good heart. You are also incredibly beautiful, funny and kind. That all adds up to the complete package and don't let anyone tell you any differently.'

He pulls me after him and my mind works hard to comprehend his words. Beautiful…. me? He has had more to drink than I thought.

The evening party is underway and more guests have arrived. There is loud music coming from the room where we ate and the lights flash, lighting up the dance floor as the guests get down to it.

Liam spies his friends by the bar and drags me over to them.

As they see us coming Edward cries out. 'Here they come. Where were you, your drinks have gone warm?'

Melissa looks at us and grins knowingly as Liam pulls me securely next to him and looks at me with pantie wetting, desire filled, eyes.

'Sorry guys, we had business to attend to. Did we miss much?'

Edward shakes his head. 'Nothing better than what you've obviously been up to. Lucky sod.'

He then punches Liam on the arm and grins at me.

Now I feel uncomfortable. Maybe we didn't think this through.

Cindy smiles and grabs my arm. 'Come on, Annie, let's go and dance.'

I smile at her gratefully and follow her onto the dance floor.

As we let ourselves go, she shouts to be heard above the music. 'You've caused quite a stir you know.'

I look surprised. 'Why, what have I done?'

She grins. 'It travelled around this wedding like a lit trail of gunpowder. Apparently, you and Liam are into all sorts of sex games and you have tainted his mind and trapped him in a sea of depravity.'

I can see her looking at my flaming wrists and grin at the envy in her eyes. 'That didn't take long for word to get out.'

She looks at me incredulously. 'So, it's true?'

I just laugh and carry on dancing. I see the disapproving stares all around me. I can only wonder what people are saying, and you know what? I don't care a bit. Suddenly, I am the scarlet woman. Miss. Notorious. I am now more interesting than I have ever been in my life before. No longer, Annie Anderson, fired wannabee Accountant, with no boyfriend and soon to be no home. Now I am Annie Anderson, sex siren, talk of the town and the envy of the world, getting down and dirty with the hottest guy on the planet. God, I love the new me; if only it were true.

Soon the rest of the guys join us and I dance with Liam like a scene from Dirty Dancing. We're both out of control and I enjoy grinding my body against his and being dipped to the floor and one time thrown in the air—yes, really!

Now I feel free. Who cares what these people think, anyway? Tomorrow I will never see any of them ever again.

After a while, we take a breather and I follow the others to the bar. As we get the drinks, the DJ announces the happy couple will be taking to the floor for their first dance as man and wife.

I watch with interest as the theme from Fifty Shades comes on. Liam looks at me and winks.

Then we watch as the couple take hold of each other and start swishing around the dance floor to the sounds of, *'Love me like you do.'*

They look so romantic and I watch with envy as they appear completely wrapped up in each other. A happier couple I have never seen, and I am mesmerised. He holds her so tenderly and gazes at her with adoration. She giggles at something he says and then he grazes her lips lightly with his.

I can't tear my eyes away and then Liam puts his hand in mine and pulls me close to his side. I just enjoy standing with him as we observe the happy couple.

Then the music changes and I watch in disbelief as he flings her across the room and she skids to a halt gracefully. He then rips off his jacket and the music changes to the theme from Dirty Dancing. She gets up from the floor and he does this weird dance move that looks as if he is having toilet trouble. His whole face screws up and he is gyrating madly on the dance floor. Charlotte, meanwhile, rips off her skirt like Bucks Fizz in Eurovision and starts weaving sexily towards him, beckoning him over to her like Sandy from Grease.

I can feel the shock all around as they start dirty dancing, in front of the stunned room. Then he pushes her away again and does this strange Saturday Night Fever dance, circling her like a gladiator as she wiggles suggestively in the middle. Then, as the music builds, she runs to him like an Olympic gymnast on a floor routine. Then she sails high in the air as he catches her and holds her aloft like the proud bearer of an Olympic torch.

I look at Liam in astonishment and then we dissolve into hysterics along with all his friends. What the hell? This is the best dance I have ever seen.

Suddenly, the music changes into the theme tune from Pulp Fiction and to my surprise the parents take to the dance floor. Now Eric is spinning Lucy around and Charlotte's dad is dipping his daughter to the floor. Then the music changes to the Monster

Munch and Eric's parents join in and they do some sort of formation dance to the sounds of the song.

Then the rest of the wedding party take to the dance floor and it's like a scene from a film. Every iPhone is trained on the spectacle, recording it for YouTube and all prosperity.

I look at Liam and he raises his eyes. 'You thought we were mad?'

I laugh as he drags me onto the dance floor and we join in with the rest of them. I even see his mother and father dancing on the side-lines. Not quite so madly, but they are packing a few moves. This is all great fun and suddenly, I am enjoying myself way more than I thought I would.

Chapter Sixteen

Two hours later and everyone's drunk. I'm having the time of my life and I've lost count of the number of guys I've danced with. Cindy wasn't wrong and word spread quickly. Now every guy here wants to experience a moment with Liam's sexually depraved girlfriend and I'm in demand.

I am now officially a goddess. I dance with guy upon guy and am revelling in my newfound popularity. Other than Liam's friends, the other girls look at me with disdain and I don't care a bit.

After a while Liam cuts in and pulls me close as the music changes tempo. He leans down and whispers, 'At last, I have you all to myself.'

I smile up at him. 'Thanks, Liam. I've had a really good time. I'm sorry about my meltdown earlier.'

He smiles. 'Don't mention it. Anybody would after what you've had to deal with. You must never take what people tell you to heart. Just remember you are amazing.'

I smile at him happily and then he pulls me off the dance floor. 'Come on, Cinderella, let's grab a nightcap.'

As we make our way to the bar, we run into the happy couple. Charlotte smiles at us and then grins at Liam.

'Hey cousin, you haven't danced with the bride yet.'

He laughs and takes her hand. 'You don't mind do you, Annie?'

I laugh, shaking my head. 'Of course not.'

I watch as they head off and Eric turns and offers me his arm. 'May I have the pleasure?'

I smile at him warmly. 'It would be all mine.'

We take to the dance floor and he pulls me tightly against him. This is odd. I feel a little uncomfortable and try to pull back a bit but his grip is like a vice. He whispers in my ear.

'You are the talk of the wedding my dear. I've heard things about you that has piqued my interest.'

What?!!! I wriggle to get a little distance between us but to no avail. Then I feel just how interested he appears to be and feel faint. Ew!!

He grinds against me and whispers. 'Ever had a fantasy about getting it on with a groom at his wedding? I could meet you outside in five minutes. Nobody would ever know.'

I feel sick and whisper as forcefully as I can. 'Get away from me, you're disgusting. Your wife that you only just declared a lifetime commitment to is over there and you've only been married for five minutes.'

He snorts. 'She knows the score. Just because we're married it doesn't stop us from having fun.'

I feel disgusted. This guy is everything Liam said and more. He is vile and I can't get away quickly enough.

He says huskily. 'Don't worry about Liam. It wouldn't be the first time we've shared the same girl.'

Now it all slots into place and with one superhuman move I push him forcefully away and scream. 'You're disgusting. Get away from me.'

I register the surprise in his eyes as I let him have it.

'Now I know why Liam hates you so much. It was you, wasn't it?'

Suddenly, the room goes quiet and I see Liam rushing over shaking his head, 'Annie, no!'

I mustn't hear him or just ignore him anyway because I scream.

'It was you who April cheated on Liam with, wasn't it? You're despicable; trying it on with another while your new wife is nearby.'

There's a shocked silence all around us and Eric splutters. 'What are you talking about, you're a madwoman?'

Liam rushes to my side and glares at Eric angrily. 'Leave her alone. She's right you are despicable.'

He takes my hand to pull me away when we hear a shaky voice saying, 'Is this true, Eric? Did you split Liam and April up?'

I see Charlotte looking at Eric with such hurt and disappointment that I almost can't breathe.

He crosses over to her and looks at her pleadingly.

'Of course not, the girls delusional. You've heard what she's like. Just because I wouldn't give it to her, she's making these lies up about me. You know me baby bear, I love you and no other.'

He turns to face us and says angrily. 'Get out, you're no longer welcome here.'

Liam's eyes flash and he goes to speak but his mother steps in.

Facing the two of us, she looks at me with a withering, hate filled, stare.

'Eric's right. You are no longer welcome here. How dare you abuse our kind hospitality and spread vicious lies and rumours about the groom on his wedding day? You should be ashamed of yourself.'

She turns to Liam and says angrily. 'And as for you, I am more disappointed in you than I ever thought possible. I didn't bring you up to treat women as sex slaves. How could you, Liam? I think it's best you both pack your bags and leave. Take a long hard look at yourselves and mend your ways.'

Liam looks around at everyone angrily. 'Don't worry we're leaving. If anyone's disappointed, it's me. I thought I belonged to a decent, loving, family, but that isn't the case, is it? From the moment we got here you have excluded Annie and made her feel unwelcome. Just because she isn't April flaming Loveday, the girl you think is perfect for me in every way. Well, let me tell you, she's not. She is evil, manipulative and rotten inside. She cheated on me so I ended it and I'm just sorry it took longer than it should have. Annie is kind, decent and beautiful. She has more beauty in her little finger than April has in her whole body.'

He turns to Charlotte. 'Eric didn't cheat on you with April, Annie got it wrong.'

I notice the triumph in Eric's eyes and look at Liam in shock. Oh no, I've done it again. I shouldn't be allowed out. How could I have ruined their wedding, without knowing the true facts?

I go to apologise but Liam pulls me back. 'Eric tried several times but April wasn't into cheating on me with a low life, sleaze, like Eric. No, I hate and detest you because of what you did on your stag night. But don't worry, I won't tell anyone; your secret's safe with me.'

He then looks around angrily and says bitterly. 'Well, this has been fun but we must be going. Thanks for the invite, I hope you will all be very happy. Come on Annie, we're obviously not welcome here.'

He turns to go and his mother shouts, 'I think that's for the best. Only come back when you apologise and get some morals.'

She looks at her husband and shouts, 'Aren't you going to say anything, Michael?'

He looks around him and frowns. 'Yes, Liam, just go. Your mother's right. You shouldn't have caused such a scene. It's best for everyone if you just leave.'

Liam looks at him angrily and his father steps forwards and whispers in his ear. Then without another word, Liam pulls me from the room.

He doesn't stop until we are safely in the lift and then leans back heavily against the mirror and stares at me regretfully.

'I'm sorry, Annie, that was awful. You didn't deserve any of that.'

I look at him in horror. 'No, I'm sorry Liam, me and my big mouth. I got it all wrong, didn't I? The trouble is, Eric did proposition me and I saw red. The things he said made me think he'd been the one April cheated on you with. He said it wouldn't be the first time you had shared the same woman.'

Liam's eyes flash, and he says angrily. 'It wasn't April. A few years ago, I was going out with a girl called Victoria Craven. She was Charlotte's best friend, and we were all quite friendly. Then one day I found her in bed with Eric. Everything exploded and Charlotte even left Eric for a while. Then he wormed his way back into her heart and she forgave

him. Not Victoria though. She was
officially ostracised and banished from their social
circles. I was surprised to hear she was coming
tonight but that was obviously just
a rumour because I never saw her.'

The lift reaches our floor and I follow Liam to our
room.

'So, what did you see on his stag night?'

As we get inside the room, Liam sinks down onto
the couch and pours us both a brandy. He looks
angry.

'Eric wanted us to go to a club he was apparently
a member of. It turned out to be a strip club. He had
laid on everything possible. Lap dancers, alcohol
and private strip shows. It was disgusting watching
him take advantage of everything on offer. It was
evident he was a regular, and he didn't seem to care
what anyone thought of him. The last I saw, was
him disappearing off with three girls and his best
friend. It didn't take Einstein to work out what they
were going to do so I left immediately. The next
day he called and threatened me saying that if I told
Charlotte he would say it was me and not him.
Every girl would back up his story and he would
cause a public scandal that would wreck my career.

I kept quiet to protect myself and I hate myself more for it as a result. I didn't want to come here this weekend, you know that. Now you know why.'

I take his hand and put my head on his shoulder. 'I'm sorry, Liam. Now I've gone and made it a whole lot worse with your parents. They think you're some sort of sexually depraved monster and I've embarrassed you in front of your friends. I should go and let you build some bridges. You could say you threw me out in disgust or something.'

Liam shakes his head and smiles sexily at me. 'What and lose the best girlfriend a guy could ever wish for? I'm not mad.'

I laugh and he pulls me against him while we sip our drinks.

After a while something occurs to me. 'What did your dad say to you when we left?'

Liam laughs softly and grins. 'He told me I was a lucky bastard.'

Chapter Seventeen

I am woken the next morning by a knock on the door. I open my eyes and stare at the gorgeous guy lying next to me and it all comes flooding back.

After we had drunk the decanter dry—again, Liam and I went to bed. Just as friends though—more's the pity. We took advantage of the soft five-star bed and just fell into a deep, alcohol-fuelled, sleep.

He's still sleeping and I get out of bed gingerly, so as not to wake him and head out to the sitting area to answer the door.

I do hope it's not his mother.

When I open it, I'm amazed to see a waiter who then proceeds to wheel a trolley into the room. 'Room service madam. Where would you like it?'

I shake my head in astonishment. 'I didn't order this; you must be mistaken.'

Then I hear. 'No, I did.'

I look around in surprise as Liam comes into the room. I watch as he hands the waiter a tip and sees him to the door.

When he comes back, he grins. 'I ordered this yesterday. I knew I wouldn't want to face anyone before we left, so ordered breakfast in bed.'

He winks and then heads over to the trolley. I join him and look with pleasure at the feast laid out before our eyes. Wow! There is more food here than I have ever seen.

Liam laughs softly and hands me a plate. 'Eat up, Annie, you could probably do with this.'

We fill our plates with Danish pastries, croissants, and fresh fruit. I pour us both a coffee and we sit on the little couch in a companionable silence.

This is nice, I'm enjoying our intimate breakfast for two. We've shut the world out and it's just the two of us in our own little cosy bubble.

As we eat, Liam grins. 'Well, last night was interesting. I have a feeling we won't be hearing the last of it for quite some time.'

I laugh. 'Sorry, Liam. It's ok for me, I don't have to see any of them again. I appear to have quite a knack for burning my bridges behind me at the moment.'

He looks interested. 'Why, what else have you done?'

I then proceed to tell him of my resignation email and he almost spits out his coffee.

'Good on you, Annie. What I wouldn't give to send a few of those myself.'

I grin and settle back, completely stuffed. 'Anyway. Now we have phase two of our operation to complete. You know, you can always back out. I wouldn't blame you.'

Liam grins. 'What, and miss out on yet more drama, with my new sex-crazed girlfriend?'

I laugh and shake my head. 'Well, only if you're sure. The trouble is, all of this will seem like a happy memory after five minutes with my family.'

Liam looks surprised. 'Why, how bad can they be?'

I just smile and look away. He's about to find out and nothing I say will prepare him for the ordeal ahead.

An hour later we pack up and ship out. Liam called us a cab and after a quick exit, we leave the wedding firmly behind us.

As we sit in the taxi, I try to steel myself for the days ahead.

Liam sighs with relief as the driver pulls away. 'Thank god for that. Now I can relax.'

I smile and feel the tension creeping over me. Silently, I pray for a miracle, please let them be normal for once in their lives.

The taxi driver looks over his shoulder. 'Where to?'

My heart sinks. Here we go. I say softly. 'Um, Riverdale Avenue, Abbotsbury.'

He nods. 'I'll have you there within the hour. You got a number for the Satnav?'

I swallow hard. 'No, just a name.'

He shouts. 'Go on.'

I sigh heavily. 'Kirrin Cottage.'

The driver laughs and Liam looks at me with astonishment. 'You're kidding, right?'

He laughs and I smile, thinking - I only wish I was.

As we head off, I decide to prepare him for what's waiting for us. I cough nervously and say quietly.

'Listen, Liam, I had better warn you about something.'

He looks interested. 'Go on, I'm intrigued.'

I sink back into my seat. 'My mother has an unhealthy obsession with the Famous Five.'

He laughs incredulously and I carry on.

'She runs this Holiday Let business from Kirrin Cottage. It goes way beyond a gimmick though. I'm called Anne for a reason and my sister Gina is really Georgina, my mum calls her George. My father sometimes refers to my mum as his little Fanny and I want the ground to open up and swallow me now because you must be wondering what the hell is going on.'

Both Liam and the driver dissolve into fits of laughter. The driver shouts. 'Sounds like spiffing fun children.'

I groan. Liam wipes his eyes and looks at me softly. 'Well, I can cope with that, Anne! It's not that bad, really. Don't worry.'

I smile nervously. He won't be saying that after a few days with them that much I do know.

Chapter Eighteen

I think we've exhausted every Famous Five joke there is by the time we pull into the Avenue.

Despite my dread, my heart lifts as I see my home rising before me, surrounded by the sea fret that clings to this coast in all its eerie splendour.

Just like in the books, a little-thatched cottage awaits us surrounded by beautiful gardens. Behind it lies the sea that sparkles on a good day. Not today though. This sea fret is ominous and matches my mood perfectly.

To the right of the house are the holiday lets that my parents run. They used to be stables and have been converted into luxury accommodation for the many tourists that flock to these parts. In total there are five of them and they are always fully booked. Not now though. It's Christmas and one thing my mother loves, even more than the Famous Five, is Christmas.

She must hear the crunch of the gravel on the drive as we approach because she flings the door open and comes running. My heart leaps as I behold my mother. For all her madness I do love her very much. She makes it impossible not to and I race from the car into her loving, welcome, arms.

Just for a moment I cling to her. I take comfort in her warm embrace and take deep breaths of her familiar perfume.

She grips me tightly and says softly, 'Welcome home, Anne. We've missed you so much.'

She draws back and looks at me, the love shining from her eyes.

I smile at her and tears cloud my view. Despite dreading every minute of what may happen, I love being here. I'm glad I came because they are just what I need right now.

I see her look behind me and then remember Liam.

Before I can even speak, she is on him like a wasp on jam.

'You must be Anne's boyfriend. I'm so pleased to meet you.'

She turns to me and raises her eyes. 'Gosh, Anne, you've done well with him, he's gorgeous.'

I roll my eyes at Liam who grins and allows himself to be led inside by my overfamiliar mother.

I follow them in and gaze around my childhood home.

Everything is still the same and I take a deep breath. Home at last.

She leads us into the living room and I'm surprised to see Gina is here already. Standing next to her by the fireplace must be her boyfriend.

Mum pulls Liam in and smiles happily. 'Look who's here. Now the family is complete.'

She turns to me and waves towards Gina and her boyfriend. 'Anne, you haven't met Dick yet, have you?'

I just stare at Gina - Dick!! You've got to be kidding me. She looks at me with a smug expression and I narrow my eyes. Dick moves across the small - now quite crowded, room and goes to shake Liam's hand.

'I'm pleased to meet you…'

Liam grins and says, 'Lia….' I quickly interrupt and say a little hysterically, 'Lian, short for Julian.'

My sister's face is a picture and I stare at her with a smug expression. There, two can play at this game.

My mother claps her hands with excitement. 'Oh, my goodness. What an amazing coincidence.'

Gina drawls, 'Yes, isn't it just?'

Liam looks at me in surprise and I smile at him apologetically.

He recovers well though and smiles around at everyone.

'Um yes, Julian. But my friends call me Liam or Lian. Either one is fine.'

Gina smiles and Dick grins around at us all. Mum takes charge and gestures for us to take a seat.

'Take a seat everyone, while I go in search of your father. I think he's fiddling with his erection in the garden. I won't be long.'

I daren't even look at Liam and Gina rolls her eyes. 'Oh, it's so good to be home.'

I look at her and we grin. She nods towards Liam. 'So, Julian hey, quick reaction. I'm impressed.'

I laugh and point at Dick. 'Dick, how original. Are we allowed to know your real name?'

He grins. 'That is my real name.'

Liam snorts and I look horrified. 'You're kidding me.'

Gina bursts out laughing and turns to Dick. 'I told you she wouldn't believe us.'

She looks at me and grins. 'Actually, it's Richard, but for obvious reasons, he agreed to go by Dick this week. Good luck with carrying on the pretence over old Ju here.'

Liam laughs and rolls his eyes. 'Well, I was warned.'

Suddenly, a little furry bundle races into the room and jumps all over me.

Liam looks at the gorgeous puppy and snorts. 'Timmy, I suppose.'

Dick laughs as I grin at them. 'Timmy number three, actually. He stems from a long line of Timmy's that have graced our presence over the years. It saves on dog tags and named pet bowls.'

Gina looks around and rolls her eyes. 'So, the Famous Five are all present and correct. Mum must be in seventh heaven.'

We hear footsteps approaching and my heart lifts as my dad follows my mum into the room. I race over to him and hug him for all I'm worth. 'I missed you, dad.'

He hugs me back tightly and whispers. 'Not as much as I missed you baby girl.'

My mum claps her hands and says loudly. 'Now, you must all be starving. I've prepared a small feast for you all and then I'll show the guys their accommodation and you girls can settle back into your old rooms. This is going to be so much fun.'

Chapter Nineteen

As usual mum has excelled herself and we eat far too much. We all fall into an easy chatter and just talk about general things for most of the meal.

Liam tells them about his photography and I skirt around the issue of my unemployment.

Gina talks about her work, which almost puts us off eating and Dick chats about the exciting world of detecting.

After we have eaten, mum stands up and smiles at the guys.

'Follow me and I'll get you both settled in. Anne and George are in their usual rooms and when you're all done maybe you can go for a relaxing walk or something.'

I smirk at Gina. As if, it's freezing out there and I think I can hear rain. No, I intend on taking Liam to the local pub for a much-needed brandy.

Liam grins at me as he follows mum and Richard from the room.

Dad drifts off back to his erection, which thankfully turned out to be the 8ft Christmas tree that my mother has insisted on in the courtyard. She has invited the local church carol singers to sing for us all on Christmas Eve, with the promise of mulled wine and mince pies, alongside a hefty donation to the cause.

I follow Gina upstairs to our childhood bedrooms. Our rooms have their own private staircase at one end of the house. We loved this as children because it was as if we had our home. The most irritating thing is I must access my room through Gina's and we had many an argument when I was banned from her room, which made life extremely difficult.

We get to Gina's room, and she dumps her cases and sinks back onto her single bed covered with a pink satin eiderdown.

She looks at me and grins. 'Some things never change.'

I laugh. 'Yes, everything seems so small now. Do you remember how big it all seemed when we were children? I mean, my flat isn't exactly big, but the rooms are a whole lot bigger than the ones in this cottage.

Gina laughs. 'I agree. My flat in Milton Keynes is quite big and much more modern than this little cottage. I do miss the place though.'

I nod in agreement.

'She laughs and her eyes flash. 'Well, I must say you've surprised me. Liam is totally gorgeous and nothing at all like I imagined. How did you land him?'

I smirk. 'Oh, you know, it was my irresistible charm and good looks that he couldn't resist.'

She laughs. 'More like you got him roaring drunk in that nightclub you're always going about. I can't imagine why he's stayed now he's sobered up.'

I pull a face and throw a nearby embroidered cushion at her.

'What about Dick? Don't tell me his name attracted you and you went out with him to please mum. You always did everything to be her favourite.'

Gina grins wickedly. 'Says you, Julian indeed. The poor guy must wonder what he's got himself into.'

She looks at me and her expression turns more serious.

'Actually, Richard and I are very much in love. It's only been three months but we already almost live together and have even talked about getting our own place.'

I smile happily. 'I'm happy for you, Gina. He seems nice.'

She looks misty-eyed all of a sudden which isn't like her at all. 'Yes, it's shocked me really. Maybe you will fall as fast for Liam and mum's dream of the Famous Five will come true.'

I smile, but my heart sinks. If only it were true. The trouble is, this time next week, Liam could be gone from my life forever. Far from living the dream, it would now appear that I'm living the nightmare. If they really knew of my situation, I wonder what they would make of it.

Guys like Liam don't end up with accountants, especially ones that can't hold down a job or a boyfriend, with the threat of eviction looming. No, Liam will head home, probably very quickly, after spending a few more days in this madhouse. He will head back to his glamorous life and probably vow never to travel by British Rail again due to the undesirables it attracts. April will beg for his forgiveness and they will go on to be a beautiful super-couple that mixes with the jet set and attends premieres and 'A-list' parties. I will watch them from my settee and dream of the few short days that I had such an amazing boyfriend.

Gina looks at me with curiosity and says softly. 'What is it, Annie? You look sad.'

I shrug and laugh nervously. 'Oh, take no notice of me. I think I'm sleep deprived. Let me dump these bags and we can find the others. I have an overwhelming urge to re-acquaint myself with the Anchor Inn.'

I know I haven't fooled my sister. She was always astute, which is why she is so good at her job. Nothing gets past her and I must try to keep my feelings in check. Nobody must know the real reason Liam is here. They would never let me forget it and tease me forever.

Leaving her behind, I head through the door in the corner of her room to mine.

It's exactly as I left it and my heart leaps, as I see my childhood laid out before me. The poster of Take That is still there with pride of place on the wall above my bed. Mr. Puddles, my childhood bear is sitting by my pillows, his arm around Winnie the Pooh and his feet on Tinky-Winky.

There are some photographs on the wall that I made into a collage detailing my school life. I look at them with a pang as I see the younger me, problem free and grinning from the photographs with innocence looking out to a brighter future.

I had it all before me. I was going to make something of my life. I always knew I wanted to ditch the sleepy little village in Dorset and experience city living. London seemed so exciting and full of possibilities. I would move to the bright lights and never look back.

It would be where my dreams of a better future would come true. My future was there among the skyscrapers. I would take London by storm and come home successful and happy. My old classmates who dismissed me and laughed about my Famous Five obsessed family would envy me and regret the day they cast me from their groups.

I would show them all. Annie Anderson would turn into a successful swan and they would boast that they once knew me and claim me as a friend.

As I pick up Mr. Puddles, I wonder how many dried tears are contained within his fur. He was my best friend. I used to snuggle up to him at night and let my hurt and anxiety pour into him. He understood. He comforted me in my hour of need. I didn't need to be popular to keep his love; I was his world and he never let me down. Here he is again, waiting to receive my grief at the realisation that I have made a mess of things once again.

I walk over to the window and look out at the misty vista. A familiar view that has transported me back in time. Back where I started with almost nothing to show for my travels.

I see Richard and Liam walking back towards the house laughing at something. Probably wondering what the hell they've got themselves into with us.

As I watch them my heart flutters. Liam Goodwin, the sexy stranger from the train who has somehow managed to capture my heart. We have become good friends and I'll miss him when he heads back to his perfect world, leaving me as memory.

Why do I always want what I can't have? I would be better off staying around here and getting a job in Weymouth. I could meet someone and settle down and live the life I was always meant to. Girls like me don't have it all. We have what life decides is right for us. Sexy, gorgeous, successful men are reserved for people like April Loveday.

Shaking myself out of my doom and gloom I place Mr. Puddles back on the bed lovingly and head downstairs to spend what little time I have left with Liam.

Chapter Twenty

The four of us head off to the local establishment. The Anchor is your typical cosy village pub. The fire is warm and welcoming, as is the landlord who smiles at the frozen strangers staggering through its doors, in need of warmth and sustenance.

Vincent has run this pub since I can remember. Along with his wife Jackie, they have served almost every person who has travelled through these sleepy shores.

Once again, my heart sings with familiarity and I smile happily at him, as he shouts.

'Look who the cat dragged in. The Anderson sisters. We haven't seen you two around here for a while. You home for Christmas?'

Gina laughs. 'For our sins. Which is why you're our first port of call.'

We all laugh and then order some mulled wine that cannot be ignored, due to the intoxicating aroma that it gives off.

We take one of the coveted seats by the open fire and sit, sipping our warming drinks and finally relax.

I watch as Gina snuggles close to Richard and feel happy that she has found love. He seems like a great guy and they are obviously very happy.

Liam shifts closer and leans down whispering, 'I don't know why you were so worried. Your family is lovely and have made me much more welcome than mine did you. You are very lucky.'

I smile. 'Yes, they are lovely. That was never in doubt. The trouble is, they are a little eccentric and not everybody understands that. Madness follows them and if you're not used to it, it can all seem very odd.'

Liam laughs softly. 'I quite like having a little madness in my life. These last few days have taught me that. Despite everything that happened at the wedding, I enjoyed spending it with you.'

His words light up my heart. He's right. Despite how awful things were, I still enjoyed myself. He is great company, and I did like his friends. Maybe I should just savour the time we do have together and make an amazing memory to tell my grandchildren.

Liam grins and pulls me close to him and we sit side by side by the open fire. We are just content to sip our warming drinks, secure in the knowledge that it's all plain sailing from here.

When we get home, my mum meets us looking extremely smart. 'Hi guys, did you have a nice walk?'

I look at Liam guiltily and his eyes twinkle. Gina nods.

'Yes, thank you; that dealt with the city cobwebs, didn't it Dick?'

He smiles and nods. 'Yes, extremely exhilarating.'

Mum smiles happily. 'Well, head off to change everyone; your father is treating us all to dinner out. His treat, with no expense spared. Dress to impress as they say.'

I look at Gina in shock. Since when could Dad afford to take us all out? It will blow their monthly budget.

Gina looks just as confused. 'Are you sure? I mean we could all chip in with the cost.'

Mum looks annoyed. 'Don't be ridiculous. It's our treat before the rest of the family descend on us tomorrow.'

Gina groans. 'Oh no, who's coming now?'

Mum looks disapproving. 'Don't be like that George. It's Christmas, the season of peace and goodwill to all men and women. The time for giving, not just receiving and charity begins at home.'

Gina rolls her eyes and I look at my mum nervously.

She smiles happily and starts ticking off names on her fingers.

'Well there's granny of course, but don't tell her I called her that.'

We laugh because my Gran is one of a kind. We must call her Lizzie because she is in denial about her age. Despite being in her mid-70s, she lives as if she's still 21. Completely up to date and embracing all the modern conveniences. She lives in a nearby McCarthy Stone community where she lives life to the full.

Mum continues. 'Then there's you, Aunt Rose and the twins, Elliott and Barney.'

Gina groans. 'Oh, not those two. We had better make the most of the peace and quiet while we can. Please say you've put them in the furthest room away from the house?'

Mum throws her a warning look and continues. 'Unfortunately, Steven is still away on the oil rigs until the New Year, so we will have to throw them a little more love than usual because they will be missing their daddy. Then lastly, we have invited Major Wilson. He was at a loose end and so we agreed he could extend his stay until the 2nd of January. I know we don't usually include the guests, but he has become more like family over the years and his son is in South Africa.'

I shake my head. Major Wilson is a nice enough gentleman, but completely deaf and as old as the hills. He is sure to grate on Granny's nerves because she can't stand anybody old, as it reminds her of her own advancing years. I can foresee many an argument and as for the twins - I share Gina's wish. Those boys are trouble, with a capital T. The fact their father is away a lot, means they are out of control and unruly. I can see lots of walks in my future this Christmas, straight down to the village pub where they aren't allowed in the resident's bar.

We all head off to change and I worry about the coming meal. Dad can't afford to wine and dine us and I sure can't afford to chip in, as Gina put it. Maybe I'll just pretend to be stuffed already and order a salad, with tap water to drink. That way I won't feel so guilty.

We are soon on our way, in the minibus that my parents use for the other part of their business.

Kirrin Cars is emblazoned on the side, advertising the bus service and tour company, that's very much my dad's baby.

While mum revels at playing the role of Aunt Fanny with her guests, my father offers a taxi service or runs tours around the Dorset countryside. It gets him out of the house and a much-needed break from my mother.

I sit next to Liam as we pile inside and dad slams the double doors shut.

I look at him and pant inside. He looks amazing as usual. Totally out of place here, with his expensive clothes and movie star looks. He sees me looking and grins. His eyes smoulder and pull me in. I could drown in those eyes and lose myself forever.

Shaking myself, I pull back to reality. I must stop these growing feelings from taking root. Liam will be gone for good in a few short days. I must picture him as Jason at all times if I am going to retain my sanity.

After resisting mum's attempts to join her in a rousing Christmas carol extravaganza, we soon reach our destination.

This can't be right! I look at Liam and he raises his eyes and his mouth twitches.

Gina voices what we are all thinking. 'What the hell are we doing here?'

Seaview Retirement Community looms up in front of us and I share my sister's dismay. This can't be right.

Mum laughs dismissively. 'We have come to their weekly meet and greet. Your father and I are regulars and they serve a fantastic three-course meal, with wine and the odd sherry for £3.50. It involves the community and gives their residents the opportunity to mix with the outside world. I must say, some of these people have led extremely colourful lives. Come on it's such fun.'

Gina isn't having it. 'For god's sake mum, this is a nightmare. Why can't we just go to the nearest Pizza

Express? I'm sure there's a voucher online we could use.'

Mum looks at her and frowns. 'Now, now, George. I didn't bring you up to be selfish. These people look forward to their weekly mingling's, and it's the least we could do, it is Christmas after all. There will probably be entertainment laid on as well. Where's your sense of adventure?'

I can see that Liam is finding it hard to hold it together and my mouth twitches as I look at him. I knew it was too good to last.

We follow them from the minivan and head inside. Gina wrinkles her nose and whispers.

'This place smells. God only knows what mum was thinking, bringing us here. If I'd wanted to drink my food through a straw, I would have gone to shake-away. They have gone too far this time.'

She stomps off, with an amused looking Dick beside her.

Liam laughs softly. 'Well, this is different.'

I grin at him. 'I did warn you. I am sorry by the way. If you ordered a cab and hightailed it out of here back to London, I wouldn't blame you.'

Liam smiles and puts his arm around me and kisses the top of my head.

'What, and miss Christmas with my new, super-hot, super-sexy, sex-crazed girlfriend, who lives life as an adventure? You must be crazy if you think I'm going anywhere.'

I grin at him. 'Well, don't say you weren't given the chance. You may regret your madness in agreeing to this.'

He laughs and we follow the others into the resident's lounge.

Seaview Retirement home is quite nice. There is a large Christmas tree in the corner and lots of fake presents wrapped up underneath. The residents sit around in high wing-backed chairs and there is a huge plasma TV, blaring out, Singing in the Rain, in black and white.

Gina is right, the place does smell. It's musty as they obviously don't allow the windows open and the smell is a mixture of stale food and bodily fluids. There is an artificial fragrance of air freshener, battling to disguise the smells, but all it serves is to highlight them even further.

The place is quite busy with other poor misguided fools, here for the cheap food. It's very loud in here, as people raise their voices in conversation with the residents.

Mum and Dad soon get swallowed up by a sea of their friends, who all appear worryingly quite at home here.

A man shouts at us from his chair in the corner of the room.

'Move out of the way, I can't see the TV. Bloody visitors, why don't you just bugger off and leave us in peace?'

One of the uniformed staff members passes by and says loudly.

'There's no need to be rude, Jack. These visitors have come to spend a little of Christmas with you. They are our guests and you should welcome them.'

Jack just looks at her angrily. 'Bloody Christmas. I hate it and all this tinsel is attracting the dust. My hay fever is out of control.'

Liam catches my eye and grins. The staff member smiles at us apologetically.

'I'm sorry, some residents get quite unsettled when their routine is altered. Some love it though as they don't often get visitors and it's like a breath of fresh air when the youngsters come.'

I feel bad and look around at the people who now call this place home. I see a lady sitting across the room smiling at us warmly and I return her smile. She beckons me over and I find myself crossing the room to sit in the seat next to her. To my surprise, Liam goes and sits next to Jack; oh well, once again he has made a strange choice.

The lady smiles at me warmly. 'Hi dearie, my name is Willow, what's yours?'

I smile happily. 'I'm pleased to meet you Willow, I'm Annie.'

She positively beams. 'Annie, what a lovely name. I had a friend called Anne once. She was a princess you know.'

I smile, as my heart sinks. This poor woman; locked in a delusional world. She has obviously lost her mind and I pity her.

Willow smiles and leans forward. 'You know, I wasn't always here my dear. I used to live in a palace. One day I was banished here and now I have many servants to do my bidding. The trouble is I can't find the King. He was to be my husband, but I think he went to war and may have been killed.'

I just murmur politely. Oh god, this is awful. The poor woman. She must have lost it.

Suddenly she laughs and punches my arm. 'Your face my dear, it gets them every time.'

I look at her in surprise as she grins. 'Sorry, I couldn't resist. My name's Ruby and my family incarcerated me in this madhouse six months ago. For the first two months, they had my picture on the door, warning visitors against letting me out. Apparently, it's against the rules to go for the odd walk on your own. It's not all bad though. At least I get to meet some decent people once a week at these events.'

I burst out laughing. 'Well, you had me fooled. So, tell me, Ruby, if you hate it so much, why are you here?'

Her eyes cloud over and I immediately regret my question.

'My family wanted to move to Weymouth to a new build house. I couldn't manage on my own anymore, so they persuaded me to sell up and move in here. That way, they could move a little further away and I would be safe and looked after. Most of the time it's not so bad. I have my friend Milly, who I hang out with and my room is clean and bright.

The staff are pleasant and organise lots of things to keep our minds active even if our bodies aren't.'

She grins ruefully. 'Don't get old my dear. It's not much fun being the last one left when your generation drop like flies. It's better to live fast and die young. At least you'll be spared from a living death.'

I feel sorry as I hear her speak. How sad. To think she is the last one left of her friends and is just waiting to join them. Now I feel more depressed than ever and hate myself for being annoyed at coming here. So, I just look at Ruby and grin.

'Hey Ruby, fancy an adventure?'

She looks at me and a spark ignites in her eyes. 'What do you have in mind?'

I grin. 'Wait there; I'll be right back.'

Quickly, I head off to find the staff member. 'Excuse me, but do you have a spare wheelchair I could use?'

She smiles and gestures to one in the corner of the room.

'Of course, where are you going?'

I wink. 'I'm going to show Ruby a good time.'

She laughs and looks at me gratefully. 'That's kind of you. Ruby's a sweetheart. She doesn't get many visitors, but always manages to stay happy and upbeat.'

I grin and wheel the chariot to my lady.

As I pass Liam, I'm amazed to hear Jack laughing loudly. Liam catches my eye and winks and my heart melts. What a guy!

I pass Gina and Richard, both sitting stiffly either side of a woman crocheting. Gina sends me the 'help me' look. I just laugh and rush back to Ruby.

Her eyes light up as I help her into the wheelchair. 'Where are we going?'

I wink. 'Take me to your room Ruby. I'm your fairy godmother and you shall go to the ball.'

Ruby squeals with excitement as we head off.

We travel down a clinical corridor where dusty silk flower arrangements reside on wooden tables. The curtains look as if they stem from the seventies and slatted blinds disguise the outside world.

Ruby directs me to her room and I'm pleased to see it's just as she described - warm and cosy.

There is a single bed, covered in a pretty duvet. One cupboard holds her meagre possessions and there are photos on every surface. I walk around the room, looking at them with interest.

Her whole life appears to be contained within the silver frames. Ruby, as a young, beautiful woman, laughing and happy. There is a wedding picture, where she smiles into the camera, with her husband standing proudly by her side.

Later, there are the family pictures, of happy times on holiday with friends and loved ones. There are up-to-date ones, of her family and grandchildren. If these photos are anything to go by, Ruby has led a very happy life.

She sees me looking at them and her eyes soften. She gazes at me wistfully.

'Where has that time gone? When I see the photos through your eyes, I can recall every second of what I was doing in them.'

I smile and point to her husband. 'He's handsome, you were a lucky lady.'

She giggles happily. 'Albert, or Bertie, as I used to call him, was one of a kind. We met when I came to Dorset to work. I was a Nanny for a lovely family at the time, and he was their gardener. We fell in love and soon had a family of our own. We stayed working for the family though and just had a cottage in the grounds. They were happy times.'

I put the frame down and look at her with interest. 'What happened to him?'

Ruby just smiles sadly. 'He died when he was in the army. It was just after the war and he was on National Service. He was posted to war-torn Germany and unfortunately, like so many before him, he never came back. The children were very young, so didn't miss him half as much as I did.'

I look at her sympathetically. 'How did he die?'

She suddenly laughs which takes me by surprise. 'Appendicitis. Not quite the hero's death, but every bit as devastating.'

She points to a picture of her family. 'I have two sons who remind me of him every day. They are my pride and joy and would have been his too if he had lived to see what they became.'

As I look at the photograph, I see two men who look very successful, dressed smartly in suits. They are standing next to two, very plain looking women, who look uncomfortable posing for the camera. I point to the photo. 'Are these your daughters-in-law?'

Ruby nods. 'Yes, they've all been married for close on thirty years each. Two more boring women you could never hope to meet.'

She laughs, as she registers my astonishment. 'They were both born with no sense of humour. In fact, they are so strait-laced, I'm afraid to speak lest I say something offensive.'

She regards me carefully and smiles. 'Word of advice Annie. Don't lose your inner child. Enjoy life and don't take it too seriously. Do what makes you happy and live life to the full. You can't re-wind a moment in life, so make every second count. Don't tread the same path as the majority and shoot for the stars. It passes by in a flash and there should be no room for regrets when you pack your bags and move into old age.'

Her words strike a chord within me and just for a moment, we stare at each other with complete and total understanding. Then, I shake myself and grin.

'Right then, we have a party to go to if I'm not mistaken. You need a smear of lipstick and then lead me to your most outrageous gown.'

Ruby laughs happily and rummages around in a drawer. She pulls a lipstick from it triumphantly and proceeds to smear her lips with the brightest red rouge.

Spying a bottle of perfume on the side, I hand it to her and she sprays it liberally. 'Got to disguise the smell of old age somehow. I'm not talking of mine though, have you smelled how stale the air is in here?'

Laughing, I look around me. 'Ok, what about something glitzy to wear? Do you have a bright scarf or a necklace that you could wear?'

She winks and whispers, 'No, but my neighbour does. She won't mind me borrowing her silver, sequined, bolero jacket. It won't be the first time.'

She beckons me over. 'Come on, wheel me next door and we'll pick it up on the way.'

Shaking my head, I look worried. 'Are you sure? I mean, it feels wrong going to someone else's room and just taking something without permission.'

She just winks again. 'Listen, dear, when you get to our age most of your possessions have either been sold or given to the family. We are all the same and so share what we have to make it seem as if we have more. Ellie won't mind at all. In fact, she headed off to her family Christmas wearing my best Burberry coat. She owes me the jacket at least.'

I shrug. 'Well, if you're sure. If the police are called then I'm dobbing you in, ok!'

She laughs. 'Where's your sense of adventure, Annie? I thought I'd met a kindred spirit in you.'

Laughing, we leave the room in search of stolen items.

Chapter Twenty-One

By the time we return most of the residents and the guests are sitting down to eat. I look around and laugh as I see Gina and Richard either side of crochet woman. They look bored out of their minds and I can tell Gina is finding this whole thing extremely irritating.

Ruby sees me looking and whispers. 'That girl doesn't know what she's missing out on.'

I raise my eyes. 'What do you mean?'

Ruby grins. 'Ava used to be a high-class prostitute. She's had more men than I've had hot dinners and the stories she tells would make your hair curl. Look at her now, Annie. She sits here most days and crochets teapot covers. I mean, who even uses a teapot anymore? I love listening to her stories, they make me feel alive.'

I look at Ava with a renewed interest. I would love to hear what she has to say, wow!

Ruby pulls at my arm and points to a gentleman sitting next to a woman who is engaging him in conversation.

'See Robert over there? He used to be a well-respected Captain in the Navy. He's been to more countries than any of us and the stories he tells are fascinating. What you see around you, Annie, are people who have lived interesting and colourful lives. They may be near the end of them but they still have so much to give. If you just take the time to listen to their stories, you would be amazed. If you then compare them with your own you would probably be found sorely lacking.'

She shakes her head sadly. 'Nobody wants to ask though. They come here out of a sense of duty and obligation. One-hour tops and they can pat themselves on the back before going back to their normal lives. Meanwhile, we are left here with just our memories and tales of a life well spent. Like I said before, Annie, don't get old, or if you do, make sure that your stories are the best ones in the retirement home. You owe it to yourself to live the best life you can.'

I guide Ruby over to the last two empty seats in the room with tears in my eyes. How she has opened my eyes today. As I look around at the people in the room, I can see what she means. The conversation is polite and stilted and the residents ignore their guests who look bored with one eye on the time. They are missing out on so much by not delving into the lives of the people next to them.

I see Liam laughing at something Jack says and my heart leaps. As he catches my eye he grins and a shiver runs through me. Ruby whispers, 'He's a fine man, don't let him go. I can tell he's a good one. Jack is difficult, and it's the first time I've seen him speak to a visitor, let alone laugh with them. Your guy must have something special because Jack is a good judge of character.'

I just smile and pick up my knife and fork. If only I had that option.

Surprisingly, the food is very good. I mainly chat with Ruby but on the other side of me is a gentleman called Cyril. He used to own a chain of pubs and the jokes he told made me blush. Gosh, no wonder my parents are regulars, who knew this place would be so much fun?

After dinner, we head back to the lounge where the staff have invited a band to play. The songs are from the fifties and my heart lifts as I watch the memories flooding back into the faces of the residents as the singer takes them back in time.

Liam joins me and puts his arm around my shoulder and whispers, 'I've had a good time, surprisingly. Jack was a rogue and you wouldn't believe what he used to do.'

I laugh as I catch sight of crochet woman.

'Oh, I don't know. I don't think anything would shock me after today. They make us look like amateurs.'

On the journey home I feel withdrawn thinking about what happened. Gina sinks back in her seat and sighs heavily.

'Thank God that's over. Mum, if you ever suggest that again then don't count us in. I mean, what on earth were you thinking? If that's your idea of fun then I'm seriously worried about you.'

Mum just shakes her head and says sadly. 'I'm sorry you didn't enjoy yourself, darling but you should have opened your mind a bit more. We can learn a lot from those people and should listen while we still have the opportunity. The trouble with the world today is that everyone is always so busy. We lose sight of what's important in life and sometimes it takes going back to the past to see a brighter future.'

I look at Liam in shock. Who knew my Mum could be so profound? Liam grins and to my surprise takes my hand in his. He doesn't say anything and we just sit together in silence for the rest of the journey home.

Chapter Twenty-Two

When I wake up the next morning, I lie in my childhood bed and savour the moment. It's good to be home, and I never thought I'd feel like that

As I glance over at the clock by my bed, I'm amazed to see it's 10.00am. Goodness, I never sleep in this late. What on earth must they all be thinking of me?

I quickly get dressed and pass through Gina's room. She's obviously up already and even her bed is made.

When I reach the kitchen there's nobody around. The breakfast things have been tidied away and there is a note on the counter.

Taken Timmy for a walk. George and Dick have gone to Exeter. Help yourself to breakfast.

As I locate the cereal, I feel bad. Goodness, I hope Liam is ok; I feel bad for leaving him.

However, it must only be five minutes later that he heads into the room. He grins at me and I notice he must have been running because he is dressed in running gear and looks a hot, sexy, mess.

He winks. 'Morning gorgeous. Sleep well?'

I laugh with a touch of embarrassment. 'Sorry, I don't know what came over me. I never normally sleep this late.'

Sitting down, he pulls the cereal towards him. 'Must be the sea air.'

I nod. 'Yes, you're probably right. Anyway, did you sleep well?'

He smiles happily. 'Yes. I'll say one thing; your parents offer very relaxing accommodation. A real home from home. I feel quite refreshed after the last few days.'

I grin. 'Probably because we've consumed less brandy. Anyway, what do you want to do today? I would recommend doing what Gina has done and get the hell out of here before the rest of the family arrive.'

Liam laughs softly. 'This should be interesting.'

I shudder. 'No, it's not. You won't think it's so relaxing when they all get here. In fact, you will be booking your return ticket quicker than you can make up your excuse to leave. Just make sure you think of one for me because I'm not sure how much more I can take at the moment.'

Liam laughs as my parents burst into the room with a very wet dog in tow.

'Oh, Annie, you're up at last. I have so much to do before the other guests arrive. I don't suppose you would help me stuff a few crackers?'

I raise my eyes. 'What on earth are you talking about?'

My mum grins happily. 'Well, Kirstie showed me how to re-vamp your shop bought crackers into highly desirable bespoke ones with just a glue gun and a few ribbons and festive berries.'

She turns to Liam and smiles. 'You know, what that woman doesn't know about Christmas isn't worth knowing. She is my Christmas guru and I wouldn't be without her books and DVD.'

I roll my eyes as Liam grins. Mum looks at us and then goes into super-hyper,
Christmas organising mode.

'Right then, Julian. You can help Kevin out with the decorations. We need them bringing down from the loft. Anne, you and I will stuff the crackers and then start decorating. The others will be here at 6 o'clock so we haven't got long. We will have to work as hard as Santa's Elves, to transform this place into a Christmas paradise for those poor children.'

I snort, 'There's nothing poor about those children.'

Mum looks annoyed. 'You sound just like George. Where's your sense of compassion? Those boys need their father and Christmas just highlights the emptiness they feel when they realise he isn't here. We must distract them at every opportunity. Now, chop, chop; like I said, we haven't got long.'

I look at Liam apologetically as he follows my mum from the room. He appears to be taking it quite well though and just winks as he passes.

The morning flashes by in a sea of glitter and Christmas carols courtesy of MTV. If I hear, 'Last Christmas' one more time, I am liable to scream by the end of it. In fact, when you come to think of it there are only a few decent Christmas songs. Every year they get rolled out and it all becomes one big trip down memory lane. Almost Christmas Groundhog Day.

I am quite pleased with my crackers. We discarded all the shop bought rubbish that was crammed inside them and replaced it with interesting jokes printed out from the Internet. We kept the paper hats but the gifts are much more interesting. Delicious Belgium chocolates for the ladies and little brandy miniatures for the men. I fully intend on grabbing myself one of those now I've been introduced to the demon drink. I may need a few shots later when the rest arrive.

I tie the last red velvet ribbon with a flourish and stand back to admire my handiwork.

Mum smiles as she looks at the glittering creations in front of us. 'There, don't they look amazing? Bought in the sale for £3 in January and transformed into expensive ones with just a little creativity and imagination.'

I smile and nod my head. 'Yes, you have excelled yourself.'

We are interrupted as Dad and Liam join us looking very hot and flustered. Dad looks at mum angrily.

'If you buy so as much as one new bauble or pre-lit twig tree then I'm moving out. Twenty boxes were in that loft and I'm just surprised it hasn't caved in. If I am killed by the ceiling caving in on me one night remember to put on my headstone - *Killed by Christmas*.'

Mum just waves her hands and looks annoyed. 'You say the same thing every year and it's getting boring. Nobody likes a Scrooge at Christmas, Kevin, just remember that. Now, we must take a room each and crack on.'

She looks at Liam and smiles. 'Julian, you go with Anne and start on the tree in the courtyard, if you don't mind that is.'

Liam just smiles politely. 'Of course not, come on Anne, let's get started.'

Shaking my head, I follow him outside.

As we start sifting through the various boxes waiting for us, I blow on my hands to try to warm them up and moan.

'Trust us to get the cold job. It's no fun decorating a tree in sub-zero temperatures.'

Liam laughs as he tries to untangle one of the many clusters of fairy lights.

'Now, now, Anne. Where's your stiff upper lip and backbone? I'm sure we will have a jolly good time decorating this super tree.'

I throw a bauble at his head and it hits him square on the forehead. He looks at me with a challenge in his eyes and soon we are throwing everything we can lay our hands on in a Christmas decoration war. This is so much fun.

I dodge around him and use the tree as cover. All manner of baubles, frosted pine cones and fake Santa's whizz past me as I return them with speed and accuracy. I almost can't breathe for laughing so hard and then we hear a window bang open and my mum yell, 'For goodness' sake children, stop messing around. They will be here soon and this place needs to be an advert for the perfect Christmas.'

Liam looks at me guiltily and we burst out laughing.

He grins. 'Have you warmed up yet?'

I nod, laughing. 'Yes, thanks. You do know I won, right?'

Shaking his head, he picks up the lights. 'I think you'll find I did, young lady.'

We grin stupidly at each other as we set about our task.

An hour later, we step back and look with satisfaction at the beautifully adorned tree in front of us. It is certainly huge and I can only imagine how magical it will look when the carol singers come to call on Christmas Eve. One thing about my mother, she leaves nothing to chance. Christmas is methodically planned down to the last home-made mince pie and I should never underestimate just how much she puts into it.

Liam looks at me and his eyes soften. 'I enjoyed that. I can't remember the last time I decorated a tree and forgot how much fun it can be.'

I nod in agreement. 'Yes, me too. Normally, mum, has it all done by the time I come. I usually try to arrive on Christmas Eve and go home the day after Boxing day. I've forgotten about the excitement that goes along with preparing for Christmas. To tell you the truth, I've become quite bored with it all the last few years.'

Liam nods. 'Yes, as a child it all seemed so magical and exciting. Now it's just a day off from work and a roast dinner.'

I smile. 'How about we finish helping them and then treat ourselves to a brandy at the pub? We will certainly need it to cope with the influx of visitors about to descend on us.'

Liam laughs. 'You and your brandy. I've created a monster.'

Worryingly, I think he is right. Maybe I should have a mulled wine instead. I don't want to get addicted after all.

Three hours later and our work is done. Liam helped my dad out with the larger decorations. The blow-up Santa that now resides in the front garden is a particular monstrosity, but a necessary one for the enjoyment of the children – apparently. Mum bought it in the sales for £10 and despite my father moaning about it, he seems very pleased now it's in situ.

We have hung wreaths and arranged festive foliage. My hands are raw from the sharp stabs of holly and I have glitter sticking to every part of me. The cards are arranged neatly in various metal holders around the cottage and candles have been strategically placed on every surface.

I think there are three Christmas trees in total. The one outside, one in the living room and one in the conservatory.

A twigged garland is wrapped around the bannisters and luxurious stockings hang from a hook on the fireplace. The whole place is adorned with a trail of fairy lights and when the last box has been tidied away and returned to the loft, we look around us with satisfaction.

The cottage has been transformed. In the dark glow of Winter, it twinkles like a beacon of light. Warm and inviting, it sparkles with promise and excitement of what's to come. This is magical and despite feeling totally exhausted, I wouldn't have missed it for the world.

Mum smiles at us happily. 'Thanks, guys, you've worked really hard. Now grab yourselves some rest before the others arrive. You've certainly earned it. I have some mince pies to make and your father is itching to retreat to his mancave. Be back by 6 o'clock to welcome granny.'

I smile at Liam as I grab our coats. 'Are you up for a brisk walk, Julian?'

He grins. 'Sure am, just lead the way.'

Mum calls out. 'In that case, take Timmy with you. He could do with a walk.'

Grabbing the lead, we head off to the warm and cosy pub.

Chapter Twenty-three

We are soon armed with our mulled wine and sitting by the cosy fire. Timmy is splayed out asleep on the floor and I look around me with contentment.

Finally, we can relax. I smile at Liam. 'Christmas sure is hard work.'

Liam smiles. 'I enjoyed it though. My parents aren't half as much into it as yours are. I forgot just how lovely it can be.'

I nod. 'Anyway, sorry about being lumbered with my Dad for the most part. I hope he didn't bore you too much about whatever it is you men talk about.'

Suddenly, Liam looks a little uncomfortable and my heart sinks. Oh no, what has he been saying?

I look at him questioningly. 'Ok, spit it out. What has my dad said now?'

Liam looks shifty, which only increases my anxiety. 'Oh, it was nothing really and I probably shouldn't say anything at all.'

I lean forward and fix him with a determined look. 'Spill all, right now. I can only apologise in advance for whatever madness has come from his lips.'

Liam sighs and takes a deep gulp of his wine. 'It's probably nothing but he kept on asking me the strangest things.'

'Go on.'

'Well, firstly he asked me what I would do if I thought my wife was having an affair.'

I lean back heavily in shock. 'What?!!'

He carries on. 'He also wanted to know my thoughts on affairs and if you suspected your partner was gay.'

I don't think I can form any words, so just look at him in confusion.

Reaching out, he takes my hand and whispers. 'Richard told me that he asked him if there were laws about reading someone else's texts. He also wanted to know if you could get prosecuted if you recorded someone without their knowledge.'

He stares at me with concern on his face.

I just laugh, slightly madly I might add, and just wave it off.

'Oh, he's probably just seen a program on the television. I know my parents and they wouldn't be involved in anything like that. Yes, that's it, he's been watching some series on the television and is thinking about it.'

Liam smiles softly. 'Yes, of course, you're probably right. I shouldn't have said anything really.'

I take another gulp of wine. Maybe I should throw in the miniature brandy that I squirrelled away from the crackers. They have burnt out most of the alcohol in this wine and I need it to help me deal with what I've just heard.

I'm not sure what we talk about for the next hour because my head is spinning with what Liam told me. Surely he's wrong. My mum wouldn't be having an affair with a woman, I just know it.

As we walk home my earlier Christmas glow appears to have evaporated and has been replaced by anxiety. Liam is also quiet and must be wondering what on earth he has walked into.

I shiver as the cold hits me. Despite being dressed for arctic temperatures it's a cold evening. Snow hasn't been forecast, just that misty rain that I could wax lyrical about for hours. I shiver and pull my coat tightly around me. Liam looks over with concern and then to my surprise puts his arm around me and pulls me close by his side. 'Come here girlfriend, you look frozen.'

My heart lifts at his words. Even though all this is pretence, there's an ever-increasing part of me that wishes it was true. I have discovered that Liam Goodwin appears to have everything a woman could wish for. Good looks, a brilliant personality, and prospects. His sense of humour matches my own and we appear compatible in every way. I know he's well out of my league though. He is a supermodel dating, hunk of a guy, who is probably regretting every second of our crazy plan. I doubt he will ever travel on British Rail again after being lumbered with me.

He interrupts my thoughts and says softly. 'Don't pay any attention to what I said earlier. I very much doubt anything is going on. It's probably as you said, he's into some drama or another. I chat with my friends for hours about Game of Thrones, and I'm hardly likely to do any of the things they do in real life.'

I snuggle in closer, making the most of this glorious opportunity and nod in agreement.

'Of course. After all, my parents live in a make-believe world most of the time anyway. Look where it's got me. Lumbered as a permanent member of the Famous Five trying to live up to their idea of the perfect family.'

Liam laughs. 'Well, there is that. Anyway, come on I'll race you.'

He starts running and I set off in hot pursuit as I try to erase what he told me from my mind. No point in worrying about it, it's not as if it could possibly be true.

Chapter Twenty-Four

We arrive home as my Gran's Fiat 500 pulls up in the drive. My heart sinks. Here we go.

The car screeches to a halt and sends the gravel flying as she does an emergency stop.

The door flies open and she emerges from her car in all her glory. 'Annie, darling. Come here you gorgeous girl and let me look at you.'

Grinning at Liam, I rush over and find myself almost crushed to death in her surprisingly strong grip.

She pulls back and I look at my glamorous Gran.

She has bleached blonde hair and bright red lips. I don't think I've ever seen her without a full face of makeup and her perfume is overpowering. She is encased in a huge fake fur coat and is wearing UGG boots.

Looking past me her eyes light up as she spies Liam standing there. 'Wow, darling, who's the hunk?'

My cheeks flame as I pull Liam forward. 'Um, meet my boyfriend Liam, gr… I mean, Lizzie. Liam, this is my gr…. I mean, Lizzie.'

Liam just smiles and kisses her on the cheek. To my complete horror, she swings her face around and his kiss plants firmly on her lips. She grabs hold of his head and presses his lips to hers and I cough nervously.

'Um, I think mum is coming.'

Granny releases a slightly disturbed looking Liam and looks around her madly. 'Where's that crazy daughter of mine?'

Luckily, bang on cue, the door opens and my mum rushes out, closely followed by my father.

'Mum, you look amazing. Have you been to that Botox clinic again?'

Granny grins happily. 'Money well spent in my opinion. You should come with me dear if you don't want people to think you're my mother. I mean, what on earth are you wearing? You really should swap Per Una for Topshop.'

Liam snorts behind me and I focus on Timmy instead. I can't look at my mother otherwise I will dissolve into fits of laughter.

Two more different people you couldn't wish to find. I sometimes think my mum is adopted because she is nothing like granny.

I am brought back to the scene as she shouts. 'Right then Kevin, unload my car and take my bags to my room. Be careful though, there are lots of valuables in there. Sandra crack open the gin; after the journey I've had I need a large one.'

She looks over at Liam and winks. 'Hey, handsome. You can come with me and keep an old woman happy. Annie won't mind losing you for a bit while she helps her mother, will you darling?'

Once again, I throw Liam an apologetic look and help my father unload the heap of bags squashed inside the little car.

By the time we have installed granny's stuff in her room, we hear another car pulling up outside.

Heading outside we see a huge Range Rover pulled up and then the peace is shattered forever. The doors fly open and all hell breaks loose.

Two little soldiers come racing out screaming at the top of their lungs. They race around the courtyard and start shooting at each other, using the Christmas tree as cover. Little foam-covered pellets spill from their nerf guns and whizz around the place like sharp stinging rain.

My Aunt Rose emerges from the car and looks at us wearily. 'Happy Christmas everyone. Sorry about this, the twins are hyper with excitement.'

They rush past us into the house and we hear granny shout, 'Bugger off outside with those guns. Are you trying to finish me off?'

Once again, they whizz past us and my Aunt grins ruefully. 'They'll calm down in a minute. They've been cooped up for too long and need to let off steam. Shall I put the bags in our room? Oh, and where do you want the presents I've bought?'

Mum shakes her head. 'Leave it, Julian can help Kevin with it after we've all had some mulled wine and mince pies. I've given you the room at the end next to the boys. I figured you would want your own room for a little peace and quiet.'

My Aunt looks at her gratefully and then sees me waiting and her eyes light up. 'Annie, darling you look amazing.'

She pulls me in for a hug just as a taxi draws up and my sister and Richard spill out.

My Aunt shouts, 'Gina, come over here you gorgeous girl.'

Gina grins and races over and soon we are all hugging our Aunt. We don't see much of her because she lives in Cornwall. In fact, we probably only see her twice a year these days and I wish it was more. We have always got on well and she has always had lots of time for us.

Mum interrupts the happy scene and takes her sister's arm. 'Come on, Rose; let's get you a drink.'

As we follow them in, I smirk at Gina.

'Well done for escaping and getting out of the decorating duty.'

She laughs and her eyes flash. 'Sorry, sis. I probably would have throttled mum with the fairy lights if I'd been here. No, Richard and I enjoyed a lovely day shopping in Exeter, followed by lunch at Jamie's Italian. You know, you and Liam should have come with us, maybe tomorrow instead?'

I look at her in surprise. 'Why, are you going back again tomorrow?'

She winks. 'Maybe, or somewhere else. In fact, anywhere but here. We may take in a film at the new multiplex in Weymouth. If we stayed here, I think I would scream.'

Shaking my head, I follow her inside. Typical Gina, selfish and intolerant. I do love her though.

Soon the little cottage is filled with life. We all sit down to one of mum's fabulous feasts and there is lots of laughing and joking. Luckily, my parents appear to have budgeted well for drinks because the wine is in abundance and I'm soon feeling quite tipsy. Here comes the lush again.

We even manage a game of charades after tea, which sends Gina into an almost near breakdown. Party games were never her strong point and I notice the wine in her glass doesn't remain there long before it needs topping up.

Granny, as usual, is hysterical. She enacts every porn film known to man, much to my mother's dismay. I daren't look at Liam, what on earth must he be thinking?

I think we all get to bed around 11 pm. The twins were banished at 9 pm and the rest of us just chilled out and drank wine while watching Christmas films. All in all, a good start.

Chapter Twenty-Five

The next morning, Liam and I are instructed to take the twins for a pre-breakfast walk with Timmy.

I look over at him apologetically and whisper. 'I told you so. It's always me that gets lumbered. Probably because Gina would lose them or something. She always gets off lightly.'

Liam laughs. 'It's fine. It's a lovely morning and a walk on the beach would be great. I'll take my camera and shoot some pictures.'

Soon we are plodding down the beach with a mad dog and two even madder children in tow.

As Liam says, it is a lovely day. The air is crisp and cold and the sky is blue. The waves crash to the shore and the seagulls cry loudly. There isn't another person in sight and despite the fact we have the twins with us, I am enjoying myself.

We watch as the boys throw Timmy's ball into the sea. The dog adores this game and doesn't appear to even feel the cold as he rushes back and forth.

Liam takes lots of photos and then fools around with the boys in the waves.

This is great, I am enjoying the fresh air. After the stifling smog of London, this is just what I need. To re-connect with nature and throw caution to the wind. Being by the sea always gives me a sense of freedom and peace. It's as though I'm on the edge of the world and nobody can touch me. All my problems are back in London and just for these few short days I can leave them behind and concentrate on a life with no worries and peace.

That peace is soon shattered when Timmy rushes up and shakes his wet fur all over me. I shriek and then the twins race over, pulling a laughing Liam behind them.

'Throw her in the sea, throw her in the sea,' they chant loudly.

I look at Liam in horror and he grins wickedly.

Before I even know what is happening, I am swept off my feet and find myself firmly planted over his shoulder as he races towards the waves. I scream loudly.

'No Liam, put me down and not in the sea!!'

He laughs and then drops me to my feet and tries to push me in the waves.

The boys scream with joy and try to help him.

Laughing, Liam shouts. 'It's ok guys, I think we got her. Maybe we should class this as a victory. You don't want to see her when she's wet and angry.'

I grin and then Barney shouts.

'You two are doing it, aren't you?'

I look in horror at Liam and his eyes flash mischievously.

I shake my head.

'Of course not, don't be silly.'

Elliott grins. 'Yes, you are, you can't fool us, it's what grownups do. When daddy is home, he and mummy do it all the time. They let us watch and everything.'

I look at Liam in horror and he tries to hold his laughter in.

'What do you mean? Of course, they don't let you.'

Barney folds his arms and looks at me knowingly.

'Well, we do. What's more, we've seen our friend's parents at it as well. Mikey says his parents are always doing it and did it in the supermarket once.'

Elliott starts chanting. 'Do it! Do it! Do It!'

Barney shouts to Liam. 'I'll take a picture with your camera if you like.'

Liam snorts and then pulls me towards him and whispers.

'I think I know what they mean. Let's give the little guys what they want.'

Then, to my utter surprise, he dips me to the floor and then kisses the life out of my lips. I hear the boys cheering and shouting words of encouragement. They soon fade into the background as I fully make the most of this opportunity by kissing Liam back with everything I've got. Christmas dreams can come true and boy is this one worth it. Kissing Liam like this is the best thing I have ever done in my life. At this moment in time, I would adopt those two little angels, who have made my wish come true.

All too soon it is over and Liam pulls me back to my feet. He smirks and I feel the colour rushing to my cheeks. Wow!

I look at the boys in total confusion, both of whom are grinning from ear to ear.

'Told you you were doing it. All boyfriends and girlfriends do and mummies and daddies, it's the law.'

I grin. 'Well, I wouldn't want to break any laws, would I?'

Liam laughs and then chases off down the beach after Barney who heads off with his camera. Timmy follows them barking madly and I smile at Elliot.

'You're all mad.'

He grins and walks beside me as we follow the others.

'So, Elliott, tell me, what do you want for Christmas?'

He shrugs. 'I wanted my daddy home but mummy said that Santa can't work miracles and made me choose from the Argos catalogue instead.'

My heart sinks at his words. Poor little guy.

Suddenly, he looks at me with a sad expression that tugs at my heartstrings.

'Ben Sullivan told me that Father Christmas isn't real. He said it was our mummy's and daddy's who put the presents down the chimney.'

I shake my head. 'Then he is very wrong; in fact, don't let Santa hear you, non-believers are put on the naughty list and you don't want to be on there.'

Elliott's eyes widen, and he shakes his head vehemently.

'Well, of course, I believe in him, so I punched him and told him he was a liar.'

I laugh to myself but make sure I look at him with a stern expression.

'If Santa saw you punching another then he wouldn't be happy. It's best just to let these things go and concentrate on being the best little boy that you can be to make your daddy proud.'

Elliot lowers his voice. 'I'm going to find out if it's true.'

I laugh and smile indulgently. 'And how are you going to do that?'

He grins mischievously. 'Well, when we sent out letters to Santa, I left one thing off. If he's magic and is real, he will give it to me.'

Suddenly, the alarm bells are ringing loud and clear in my head. Elliot carries on.

'I asked him for daddy to come home. I said a prayer to him in assembly. God won't mind that I talked to Santa instead of him, will he?'

I look at his little anxious face and my heart melts.

'No, of course not. I believe they are good friends, so you'll be fine.'

He looks relieved. 'If he can't bring my daddy back, I asked him for Bubblehead Barbie instead.'

I stop in my tracks. What?!!

He laughs and stares at me with the eyes of the innocent.

I say somewhat nervously, 'Um, why would you want a Barbie doll anyway, Elliott?'

He grins. 'I heard Macie Green telling Emma Matthews that she would do anything for Bubblehead Barbie. If Santa brings me one, I'm going to give it to her if she'll do it with me.'

I feel quite relieved at his words, no matter how disturbing they are.

We are interrupted as Timmy runs back and jumps up at me with wet, sandy, paws.

Liam and Barney follow laughing and I look at Liam with terror-filled eyes.

As Barney pulls Elliott away to jump the little sea pools that have appeared in the sand, Liam looks at me and raises his eyes.

'What's up? You look as if you've seen a ghost.'

Quickly, I tell him what Elliott said and he frowns.

'That's ok, we'll just go to town later and get one. We were going shopping anyway.'

I breathe a sigh of relief. Of course, how stupid of me.

If we can't rustle up his daddy, then I'm sure as Santa's Elves, that I can manage a Bubblehead Barbie.

Chapter Twenty-Six

When we returned to the house another guest had arrived. Major Wilson, is one of my parent's regular guests and he is a very smart man in his 70s. He looks quite distinguished, with silver hair and smart clothes. He is as deaf as a post though, so we must shout at him to make him understand.

He smiles as we head inside.

'Good morning, Anne. How lovely to see you again.'

I smile and kiss him on the cheek. 'Major Wilson, have you met Liam?'

As they shake hands, my mum looks at me in surprise.

'I thought you called him Lian, short for Julian?'

I recover quickly. 'Yes, sometimes he gets called Liam, sometimes Lian. I told you that. Liam is my… um… pet name for him.'

My mum looks surprised. 'Not very original, darling, if I must say.'

I just shrug as Liam tries not to laugh.

Granny comes in and rolls her eyes as she sees the Major, before plastering a sickly-sweet smile on her face.

'Major Wilson, how lovely to see you again.'

His eyes light up as he sees granny in her ripped at the knee's jeans and sequined jumper.

'Elizabeth, how lovely you look as always.'

She waves her hands in irritation.

'Yes, yes, enough with the pleasantries. You need a drink young man. Fancy accompanying me in a small sherry before breakfast?'

Liam snorts and Major Wilson looks surprised. 'Well, it's a bit unorthodox, but why not? It is Christmas after all.'

We follow them into the dining room and see the feast awaiting us. Kirrin cottage is always booked for a reason and it's this breakfast. Mum takes her Aunt Fanny duties extremely seriously and has conjured up a five-star breakfast feast.

Cereals, fruits, and yoghurts, jostle for position with crusty rolls and every variety of preserves.

The smell of bacon is wafting through the cottage and my stomach growls.

Liam grins and we settle down to devour as much of it as is humanly possible. Thank God I live away from home. I would be the size of a house if I didn't.

The twins fight over a sausage, as Gina and Dick join us. The only one absent is my father.

Mum comes in from the kitchen and shouts over to me. 'Run down to the mancave, Anne and fetch your father. He won't want to miss breakfast.'

Sighing irritably, I set off to find him.

Dad's mancave is the proverbial garden shed that it would appear every man covets at some time or another. It is far enough away from the house to class as an escape, but near enough to pop home for a bacon sandwich and a pot of tea.

I hurry down the path cursing my bad luck. If they've eaten everything before we get back, I'm liable to throw a tantrum.

I soon reach the door and contemplate kicking it in, before deciding to just knock on it loudly before venturing inside.

Unlike most men's sheds, this one has been kitted out as an office. As I enter my father looks up and snaps his laptop closed - a little guiltily as it happens.

His eyes soften as he sees me and he smiles. 'Have you been sent to get me, honey?'

I nod. 'Yes, it's all ready. We had better hurry up before there's nothing left.'

He smiles and we head off back to the house.

As we walk, he coughs nervously and says, 'You don't mind me asking you something, do you darling?'

I look at him nervously and shake my head. 'Of course not, what's on your mind?'

He looks thoughtful. 'Well, say you received a credit card statement, and it showed a holiday for two in Barbados. Would you question it, or just think that it was your husband planning a nice surprise for you?'

I shrug. 'I don't know, really. I suppose I would keep quiet if I'm honest. Although, I may contact the travel company on the pretext of checking the itinerary, just so I knew the details.'

He nods in agreement. 'Yes, I thought the same. Thanks, darling, you're a good girl you know.'

As we head inside, Liam's words come back to haunt me. I hope that things are ok with my parents. Something is going on and it doesn't take the Famous Five to work that one out either.

As we head inside, I cringe as my father puts his arm around my mother and says lovingly. 'There she is, my little Fanny.'

I look over at Gina and she looks as mortified as me. Liam and Dick are grinning and I sink into my chair and stuff a croissant quickly in my mouth. I need comfort food and fast.

After breakfast, Liam, Gina, Dick and I head off to town to do some Christmas shopping. We need to grab some gifts and it's our only opportunity before Christmas Eve.

We borrow the Kirrin wagon and set off with Gina at the wheel.

Soon we arrive in Weymouth and discover that everyone else has the same idea.

It must take us half an hour to find a parking spot, and we only manage that because Gina reversed at 30mph to beat a Volvo to the last remaining space.

We decide to head for the nearest toy shop. Bubblehead Barbie is first on the list.

The crowds are out in their droves and there is a general buzz of excitement that last minute shopping brings. Santa's stand on street corners with charity buckets and Christmas carols blare out from large speakers. Luckily, it isn't raining, and the sun is shining brightly in the sky.

Here we are. The calm before the storm – or is it the other way around?

After the third toy shop, I am losing the will to live. It appears that Bubblehead Barbie is the, 'must have,' toy of the season. Everywhere is sold out with no hope of a delivery. I gaze at the shop assistant in frustration and she shrugs.

'Listen, why don't you try Bensons. They have a toy department and I know they have deliveries on Thursdays. They may have had a batch in.'

I almost kiss her and grab Liam's hand. 'Come on, let's go. We've no time to waste.'

Gina and Dick follow closely behind and we head off to Bensons.

I remember this shop from my youth. It is a family run department store, stuck firmly in the past.

Carpet disguises the floor which has seen better days and the fixtures are yellow and dusty.

The buyers obviously haven't changed, because the clothing is for the elderly, which would make granny throw her hands up in horror.

We head up the escalators to the toy department and look around wildly for Barbie. All I can see is an empty display and my heart sinks.

Liam smiles reassuringly. 'Come on, let's ask the sales assistant. They may have some in the stock room.'

We join the queue and Dick and Gina carry on looking around the department.

The line is long and there are lots of disgruntled customers waiting. By the time we get to our turn, I am feeling super anxious. The assistant smiles and I fix her with my most beseeching look.

'Excuse me, but we are looking for a Bubblehead Barbie and I was told you had a delivery today.'

I hold my breath as she looks thoughtful.

'I think we just sold out. There may still be one in the stock room, I'll check.

I smile at her and say somewhat hysterically.

'Oh, please try to find one. A little boys Christmas spirit depends on it. If Santa doesn't deliver then Christmas will be ruined for him forever.'

The assistant edges away, shooting me a worried look as she goes.

I tap my foot nervously and the lady behind me taps me on the shoulder.

'Good for you dear. We need more parents like you who don't conform to the typical stereotypes for their children. If your little boy wants to play with Barbie then good on him.'

Startled I shake my head. 'Oh no, it's for…'

Liam quickly interrupts. 'Thank you, we pride ourselves on our forward thinking. There are no pink and blue restrictions in our house.'

The woman smiles and I look at him in shock as he shrugs. Maybe he was right to interrupt. Telling the lady she was a gift for a girl in return for doing it with a six-year-old boy, may have caused some concern.

The assistant returns empty-handed. 'I'm sorry, madam. They have all sold. I'm so sorry.'

I look at Liam with panic filled eyes. As I turn away, I suddenly spy a woman walking past with the distinctive packaging of Bubblehead Barbie in her bag.

Quickly, I grab Liam's hand and follow the woman, whispering softly.

'Look, see that woman in front of us. She's got Bubblehead in the bag. Don't take your eyes off her while I think of a plan.'

I wave Gina and Dick over and we follow the woman outside.

She heads out onto the High Street and Liam whispers, 'What next?'

Gina looks at Dick. 'Over to you detective.'

Dick looks thoughtful. 'We'll follow her and come up with a plan.'

I look at him and roll my eyes. 'Good plan, Sherlock.'

She soon heads to a nearby Costa and Dick says in a low voice.

'Right, here's the plan. It's obvious we need to play this one carefully. The only thing to do is deploy our best weapon.'

We all turn to look at Liam, who frowns. 'What me? Why, what can I do?'

Dick says softly. 'You need to engage with the target. Talk to her, find out her weakness and then exploit it. You must find a way for her to give up the prize. The rest of us will split up. Annie, you cover the door so if she leaves, we don't lose her. Gina, you sit at the back of the shop and report what you see. I will cover the side area and between us all we'll have her covered.'

He looks around. 'Has everyone got it?'

We nod and take up our positions. Trust me to have to wait by the door. It's freezing here.

Liam joins the queue for the drinks and Dick follows a little way behind. Gina heads to the rear of the shop and I sink into a seat by the window, grabbing a complimentary newspaper to hide behind.

I watch as Liam grabs his drink and follows the woman to her table. I can't see his face, but watch as her eyes light up as he says something and sits down in the seat opposite her.

My phone flashes with a text from Gina.

'Mission underway. Operative in place and target engaged.'

I type back furiously.

'Really, Gina???'

My phone buzzes again. This time from Dick.

'Target is laughing at something the operative is saying. Conversation has been struck up, and all is going well.'

I sink back in frustration.

Please get the doll, Liam, I silently chant. It's so important that Elliott doesn't lose his belief in Father Christmas. As soon as the magic goes, Christmas is never the same again. Children should hold on to that for as long as possible. I can't help with his daddy, but if I must wrestle that woman to the ground for Bubblehead Barbie, I will.

My phone buzzes again.

'Target laughing and gazing into operative's eyes. Looking good.'

I feel a flash of annoyance. How dare that woman flirt with my pretend boyfriend? Doesn't she know that he's temporarily taken? Goodness, I can't let him out of my sight for one minute before the hordes are in hot pursuit.

This time Gina buzzes.

'Oh my god, Bubblehead in view, I repeat, Bubblehead in view.'

I feel the excitement stirring and crane my neck to watch. All I can see is a man eating a muffin blocking my view.

I sink back again in exasperation. The suspense is killing me.

Dick buzzes.

'Operative has hands on target, I repeat hands on target.'

What?!! Is Liam really touching that scarlet woman in full daylight? I've heard of taking one for the team, but this is getting ridiculous.

Once again, the phone shatters my panicked thoughts. Gina texts.

'Captive has been exchanged for business card. I repeat, captive been exchanged.'

What does she mean business card? Why is Liam arranging to communicate with this woman outside of the operation? Why? Why? Why?????

Suddenly, I see Liam walking towards the exit holding the coveted doll. As he passes, he flashes me a triumphant look and carries on out of the door.

Quickly, I scrape my chair back and follow him outside. Gina and Dick are in hot pursuit and we head off towards a little side street beside the Costa.

As I turn the corner, I can't see Liam and step up my pace. Where is he?

Suddenly, I am pulled into a shop doorway and look in surprise at the grinning, extremely smug, face of Liam.

'Here you go Santa; your wish is my command.'

He thrusts Barbie at me and a huge grin spreads over my face just as the others catch up with us.

Gina laughs and pats Liam on the back.

'Well done Poirot. Perfectly executed I must say.'

Dick grins. 'She was putty in your hands as soon as you sat down. What did you say?'

I look at him with interest and he smirks, obviously loving his moment of fame.

'I just struck up a conversation with her. I told her that I was looking for Bubblehead for my niece, who I adore. I had promised it to her for being good all year, but was going to have to disappoint her.'

I shake my head. 'Is that it? You could have made up a better story than that. I mean, a terrible illness would have been good, or a parent leaving, or being bullied at school and Barbie would be her only friend. Come on Liam, that's lame.'

Liam raises his eyes. 'It worked though, didn't it?'

Gina prods me in the ribs as Dick grins.

'I saw you exchange numbers though. What's the story there?'

Liam shrugs. 'I told her I was a photographer for Vogue and she got quite excited. She wouldn't let me pay for Barbie, but said I could return the favour by taking some Art shots of her and her husband for their newly re-modelled house in London. Apparently, she is down here at their seaside retreat for Christmas. As she put it, her friends would be green with envy when she told them.'

I shake my head. 'What's an Art shot when it's at home?'

Liam looks slightly uncomfortable.

'Nude, I believe. She wants some tasteful images of her and her new husband to adorn her bedroom walls.'

Dick snorts and Gina looks interested. 'Cool, can I be your assistant?'

I throw her a, disgusted of Dorset, look.

'That's horrible. Why on earth would people want naked pictures of themselves plastered all over their walls? Ew!'

Liam laughs. 'It takes all sorts, Annie. Anyway, haven't we got Christmas presents to buy? Time is running out.'

I look at the time on my phone and grin. 'One hour, plenty of time.'

I turn to Gina. 'Lead me to Poundland dear sister.'

She laughs and the guys look surprised.

Gina grins. 'Family tradition. We can only spend £1 and it must be something useful. We all place our gifts in a large Santa's sack and it becomes a lucky dip. If you want you can swap what you get with someone else. It's quite fun really. Now, I will need to buy eleven gifts if I've counted right.'

Dick looks surprised. 'Why eleven, I counted ten?'

I interrupt. 'Timmy, of course. You can't leave him out, it isn't fair.'

Liam laughs and grabs my hand; this should be fun.

Chapter Twenty-Seven

Armed with our purchases we head home to wrap them. All of this has been exhausting and I slump against Liam in the back of the minivan.

He puts his arm around me and I enjoy the journey home way more than I should. I really must try picturing him as Jason again. We are growing closer by the hour and I know I'm in for a big disappointment when we return to London.

At least he's mine now, though, and I fully intend on making the most of the last few days we have together, before he returns to a jet-set life and I to the job centre.

When we get home, I hide Barbie in my room and stuff the gifts under my bed. I will wrap them after dinner.

We settle in for the evening and watch Elf on TV. This is my favourite film and I laugh harder than the children at his escapades. I can feel Liam watching me from time to time and wonder if I'm overdoing it a bit. The trouble is, I never have managed to ditch my love of a good children's film and coupled with the Christmas theme I'm in seventh heaven. He must be so bored. I mean, he's used to mingling with supermodels and celebrities. Now he's mingling with the insane in a re-make of the Famous Five.

I notice that Granny and the Major are getting on quite well. They are laughing together over a game of cards and I smile to myself. It must be nice for her to have some company. My mum is always crazy, xmas mum and is busy fussing about doing a million things at once in her quest to deliver the perfect Christmas. Dad is always, and I mean always, in his mancave, doing god only knows what.

Suddenly, the worry returns and I think about what Liam told me, coupled with my own strange conversation. Maybe I will do a little more digging for my own peace of mind of course.

Jumping up, I go in search of my mum who's in the kitchen, apparently dipping peppermint creams into chocolate.

'Hi Anne, would you like to help me assemble the table presents?'

I smile and join her at the counter.

In front of me are little boxes lined with doilies. She has made some lovely peppermint creams and is decorating them with chocolate and crushed nuts, before placing them carefully in the boxes ready for decoration.

I help her dip and she smiles happily. 'I love these times. Creating little gifts of happiness brings me so much joy in the festive season. It's these little touches that make Christmas special, don't you agree?'

I nod and smile warmly at her. 'How are you both? It's been so hectic since we arrived, I haven't had much of a chance to catch up.'

She smiles happily. 'We're fine, thanks darling. Life has been good to us. The business is thriving and we have many varied interests.'

Silently, I worry about those interests and delve a little deeper.

'So, tell me what you're into these days. Last time I came it was badminton.'

She grins. 'Oh, nothing, just the usual. I have my crafts and my guests. Your father has his mancave to amuse him and we just muddle through life as best we can.'

Ok, I'm getting nowhere. I need to investigate further.

'Hey mum, shall I take dad a cup of tea and some mince pies? He's been out there for hours.'

Mum smiles. 'Of course, darling. You are so good, you know that.'

I nod, as she flicks the kettle on.

'So, tell me about Julian. How did you two meet? I like him by the way, you're good together.'

Feeling uncomfortable, I stick to the agreed plan.

'Well, we met at the local nightclub. We kind of hit it off and have been dating ever since.'

I am suddenly very interested in the task in hand. I hate lying to my family, but they would be horrified if I told them I had picked him up on the train after he got me drunk and then took me to a family wedding.

Luckily, I'm spared from more questions as the kettle boils and mum makes the drink.

As I walk towards the mancave I wonder what I'll discover?

Once again, it's a frosty night and the night air chills my bones as I walk the short distance to find my father. Little fairy lights adorn the trees and it all looks extremely magical. I hear an owl hooting nearby and the gentle rustle of the trees as the wind catches them. Even the moon is out in force tonight and casts little shadows on the ground as I walk.

The hot steam from the tea escapes into the atmosphere and the heat from the mug warms my hands.

I reach the mancave and knock hesitantly on the door.

'Come in, whoever you are.'

Smiling, I push my way inside. Once again, dad is on his laptop and I notice he immediately closes the lid when I enter.

'Ah, Anne, how lovely. Armed with sustenance if I'm not mistaken.'

I nod and place the mug down in front of him, then retrieve the mince pies from a little freezer bag in my pocket.

'So, what keeps you locked away in here when Elf is on the TV?'

Dad laughs. We always watch Elf together because he is just as much a sucker for a Christmas film as I am.

He looks a little uncomfortable and just waves dismissively.

'Oh, just the accounts. You know your mother; she pours a small fortune into Christmas every year.'

I look worried. 'You're ok for money, aren't you? I could look at your accounts and see if I can help you save anything.'

Dad smiles and shakes his head. 'No, we've got it all covered thanks. As you mention accounts though, out of interest, what would your advice be if a couple had a joint account and one partner appeared to be withdrawing large amounts of money from it with nothing to show for it? Would you demand the receipts and make a scene, or would you just keep quiet and see what happens?'

Ok, this is getting weirder by the day and I'm now extremely worried.

I shake my head. 'I would confront them. I mean, it's both your…. their money and you would have a right to know where it's going. It may be just a surprise treat, but even so, something isn't right there.'

He looks thoughtful. 'Yes, I think the same. Anyway, let's get back to the fire. I can feel a Christmas tipple calling my name and if I know your mother she will have organised some game or another.'

I follow him out and look back at the computer residing innocently on his desk. There it is, the holder of the secrets that my father is keeping. I must find out what they are before I'm driven mad with worry.

Dad wasn't wrong about my mother and when we get back to the house, she calls us to attention.

'Right then. I have organised
a Christmas scavenger hunt in the garden. There are eleven gifts hidden around it and you must all find one and bring them back. The person who gets the most wins a special prize. Everybody gets a prize, but the winner benefits from two. You have thirty minutes to find them. Now, on your marks, get set, go!'

The twins run from the room like greyhounds from a gate. Gina pulls Dick behind her and they are off and running. Granny teams up with the Major and I expect her fluorescent orange jumper will be of some benefit in the darkness. Liam grabs my hand and grins.

'Come on girlfriend. I don't like to lose, so game on.'

Laughing, I follow him from the room.

All around us is complete and utter chaos.

There is lots of screaming as people find the desired parcels that are stuffed into bushes and hanging from trees. The moon acts as a torch, working alongside the various phones that are beaming out light to locate their targets.

I spy Gina and Dick snogging behind a tree and grin to myself. They are so good together. He is perfect for her and appears to take everything in his stride. I'm glad she has found someone like him.

Laughing, I run around the garden with Liam, like two crazy elves. We push the others out of our way and grab hold of any brightly wrapped packages that we see. All in all, when the whistle blows, we have found three. Liam two and me one.

As we head inside, Liam grins. 'That was fun. Do you do this every year?'

I shake my head. 'No, sometimes we play a game and sometimes we go out. I think she did this for the children. Mum will be going overboard to make this an exciting Christmas for the twins. She's always been good at that and is probably loving every minute of it.'

Liam laughs and I watch as the moon lights up his face. He is so gorgeous. Well out of my league and a part of me feels sad that he will soon be gone from my life. As if he senses my thoughts, he stops and pulls me around to face him.

Just for a moment, all noise fades into the background. It's just me and him, standing in the frozen garden looking at each other with confusion. He stares at me and I him. He leans in and whispers.

'Thank you, Annie. I'm glad we met on that train because I'm having the best Christmas I can ever remember having. I just want you to know that and hopefully it will just be the start of a beautiful friendship.'

I smile, but focus way too much on the word friendship. I feel the disappointment crashing over me at his words. Friends, of course. I must have been stupid to ever think it could be more than that. Pushing my disappointment firmly down, I just smile and shiver.

'Of course, it will. I have enjoyed every minute of our adventure so far and will look forward to many more in the future.'

The twins barge past us and pinch a gift from my hands. They race off laughing and Liam grins.

'Come on, lets' get em.'

Laughing, we race off after the boys, now firmly focused on revenge.

The rest of the evening is spent drinking and chatting. Dick is great fun and I watch Gina and Liam getting on well. I keep a sharp eye on mum and dad, but all seems ok, so I push my worries aside.

Granny comes over and whispers. 'I like Liam, Annie. He's a good one. Make sure you keep hold of him. You're a lucky girl and if you like I'll cover you later if you want to sneak away to his room for some fun.'

I stifle the slightly hysterical giggle threatening to emerge at the thought of sexy fun with Liam in the dead of night. If only. Instead, I just smile and hug her beside me.

'Thanks, Lizzie. I'll be fine. We can keep our hands off each other for a few more days.'

Granny looks at me thoughtfully. 'Don't keep him at arm's length too long, Annie. My advice for a happy relationship is lots of sex, often and in as many ways as possible. Keep the mystery going and surprise him occasionally. Don't get boring in bed and you will have a happy life.'

She heads off to replenish her sherry glass leaving me feeling very hot and bothered. Sex advice from your gran. Ew and double ew.

Chapter Twenty-Eight

As soon as I wake up the next morning the excitement grips me. Christmas Eve! How excited am I? I always love the day before Christmas. There's a sense of anticipation that never seems to disappear, no matter how old you become.

My thoughts are interrupted, by a strange noise coming from Gina's room.

Sitting up, I strain to hear and process the sound. If I didn't know better, it sounds as if she's getting down and dirty with Dick!

I hear her moan, then gasp and just stare in front of me in shocked disbelief. Surely not, she wouldn't... oh my god, she most definitely is!!!

I can't believe it. In her childhood bed, not a stone's throw from her sister. Ew, I can't bear it.

Her grunts and moans fill my ears as I put my hands over them, trying to block out the sounds of intense sexual activity.

I am trapped in my room because the only way out is through hers. This is a disaster. Surely, she wouldn't do this to me. I feel sick!

I drag myself miserably over to the window. Maybe I can jump out? I don't know, shimmy down the apple tree like they do in American movies.

The trouble is, we don't have any trees or drainpipes outside my window. Just the remnants of the ivy that my mother made my father strip from the walls as it invaded the house.

The sounds get louder and I wonder what on earth she was thinking of? I mean, in her own home with her parents nearby. How disrespectful. Why couldn't she go to Dick's room for god's sake? This is terrible.

I look out of the window in anguish. How long can they possibly go on for? And what happens when they finish? Am I supposed to look at them as if I never heard anything? She's so selfish, what a cow!

Then everything changes as I spy a familiar person walking down the path towards the house. What the hell, Dick?!!

I do a double take. This can't be right. If Dick's out there then who on earth is Gina getting down and dirty with in her single bed for one?

The shock hits me before the nausea. There can only be one culprit – Liam!

I can't believe it, how could they? It's bad enough catching my real boyfriend in another, but the thought of my pretend one inside my sister is devastating on so many levels.

I want to cry and race in there, pull them apart and batter them both to an untimely death. How could they do this to me and Dick? There is no rational explanation and the hate I'm feeling is threatening to overwhelm me. That's it, Christmas has been ruined for me - forever!!

I throw my head under the pillows to drown out the sound of my hopes and dreams of three days crashing around me. We had a future; we were happy and in love. For one more day anyway. Poor Dick, he will be devastated.

What happens when Gina and Liam become engaged and I will have to go to their wedding? I will be a bridesmaid at the wedding of the man I love.

Suddenly, I sit bolt upright. What did I just say?

I sink back against my pillows as the realisation hits me. Somehow, during the last few days my heart has been claimed by the sexy stranger from the train. Everything we have done flashes before my eyes. His smile, the way his eyes light up when he laughs. The little touches he gives me when I least expect it. A reassuring hand on mine when I need it most. A smile and a laugh drawing me in. The way he cared for and protected me against his family and friends. Even the way we fought like children in a gentle teasing manner. All of that has added up to one massive hole in my heart that has been replaced by disappointment and anger at the fact that he is now next door screwing my sister.

As if to reinforce the fact, I hear his guttural moan accompanied by hers and then there is silence. Total and complete silence. Not a bedspring groaning underneath their weight, not a sigh of contentment and not a gentle whisper of endearment. Nothing.

In fact, are they even still there?

What am I supposed to do now? How can I go down to breakfast and act as if nothing has happened? This is a nightmare. For this to happen to me twice, in almost as many days, is catastrophic.

My misery is now off the scale. My pretend boyfriend and my real sister. I feel empty inside. Wrung out and an emotional wreck. There is only one thing I need now – Mr Puddles!

Mr Puddles, is now living up to his name, as I pour my entire supply of tears into him. It's not fair.

I know that Liam is well and truly out of my league, but I had been living the dream, despite it being a pretend one.

Trust my sister to spoil it for me. She always wanted what was mine. It started with the dolls I got for birthdays and Christmas. She would work out a way to swap them for her bits of old tat. Then she tried to take Timmy's affection away from me, that is, Timmy number one.

If I did well at school, she did better. If I was complimented on my appearance, she would go one better and take the attention away from me onto her.

She even managed to get a better Saturday job than me. I worked in the local farm shop and she became employed at the local dress store. And now this. My perfect boyfriend has been rustled out from underneath my nose, with not a thought for Richard and me.

Suddenly, the despair changes to anger and a cold feeling creeps over my heart, hardening it forever.

I will not put up with this, Christmas or no Christmas. This time I will win.

Chapter Twenty-Nine

With determination I set off downstairs. I try to avert my gaze from Gina's bed as I cross through her room. The last thing I want to see is any evidence of their passion.

I feel really hurt and upset. I know that Liam is only doing me a favour and I have no right at all to be jealous, but I can't help myself.

With a heavy heart I enter the kitchen and am relieved to see that it's empty. The only life form in the room is Timmy and my eyes mist over as he wags his furry tail and comes across to give me a welcoming kiss.

Patting him on the head, I decide a brisk walk by the sea is in order to mend my broken heart. So, I quickly grab his Cath Kidston lead, along with my coat and boots and head off to sea.

As I stomp down the path, I see the Major in the distance looking very pleased with himself.

He gives me a hearty wave and I just smile and return the favour. How lucky is he not to have the weight of the world on his shoulders?

As I head towards the gate at the end of the garden, I hear somebody calling my name.

'Annie, wait up!' Looking around, my heart sinks as I see Liam steaming towards me.

Seemingly out of breath, he draws near and pants, 'Wait for me. I could do with getting away from here for a bit, your family is exhausting.'

My eyes widen as I take in his flushed cheeks and tired eyes. He looks like he's run a marathon and the anger takes hold. Fixing him with a furious frown, I snap. 'I can't believe you, Liam. How could you? I know you don't owe me anything, and are free to do whatever you want, but how could you do that to Dick? I'm so disappointed in you and think you should leave.'

He just looks at me in confusion. 'What are you talking about, Annie? I don't understand. What have I done?'

I round on him angrily, as Timmy sits quietly looking between us with interest.

'Don't play the innocent with me. I heard you this morning. I must say, it was bad enough watching my real boyfriend being unfaithful in front of my eyes, but it is too much listening to my fake one having it away with my sister in the next room. Not to mention the fact she's practically engaged. You both disgust me.'

I turn away, my tears threatening to blind me.

Then I feel him pulling me around to face him and I see the hurt and confusion in his face.

'I have no idea what you are talking about. I haven't even seen Gina since last night and all I've done this morning is help your mum unpack the home delivery. She must have bought out the whole supermarket and I'm exhausted.'

I stare at him in horror. He stares back and immediately I know he is telling the truth. I let the news digest for a while and then look at him and shake my head. 'If it wasn't you, then who was it?'

Liam looks concerned. 'Listen, let me grab my coat and I'll join you. Tell me what you heard and we will work it out.'

I nod as he races back to his room to grab his coat. As I stand here in the frozen garden, my mind is racing with what has happened. It doesn't make sense.

By the time, Liam returns, I have worked myself right up.

He looks at me with concern and takes my hand. 'Come on gorgeous, let's sort this out.'

As we walk down the path towards the beach, I tell him what I heard. He looks at me in disbelief and shakes his head.

'You must be mistaken. She could have been watching the television or something.'

I look at him with wild, crazy, eyes. 'There isn't a TV in her room, and I know the sound of my own sister moaning. God only knows I've had to put up with it one way or another all my life.'

Liam looks uncomfortable. 'Um, maybe she was… you know… um... going it alone.'

'Ugh, Liam, stop, of course, she wasn't. I heard a man's pleasure in that room as well as hers. She was most definitely not alone.'

Liam looks thoughtful. 'And you definitely saw Richard during this sordid act.'

I roll my eyes. 'It's not funny, Liam. I know what I heard and there can only be two possibilities. Before you say anything, I don't want to hear them out loud, ok?'

Liam nods and I can tell he is finding this rather amusing.

I sigh heavily. 'I did see the Major looking very satisfied with himself. You don't think Gina has a thing for older men, do you?'

Liam starts laughing and I feel cross. 'Shut up, Liam, this isn't funny. You know, as mysteries go, this is one I never thought I'd have to solve. I must have missed the Famous Five book when George goes behind Dick's back and gets it on with Uncle Quentin.'

Liam is laughing uncontrollably now and wiping his eyes says, 'There really is only one thing we can do.'

I sigh heavily. 'Ok, what?'

He grins. 'We will have to call in the Secret Seven as back up.'

That's enough and I launch myself on him like the wronged woman that I was ten minutes ago. We end up engaged in a huge play fight on the beach and Timmy joins in barking and pulling on our coats.

By the time Liam wrestles me to the sand, I'm really enjoying myself. Who'd have thought, the idea of my father or the Major, in bed with my sister would result in me having my dreams come true. My sexy stranger from the train, on top of me on the sand, holding me down and looking at me strangely.

Suddenly, his expression turns a lot more serious. He reaches up and tucks a stray piece of hair behind my ear and his eyes soften drawing me in.

I stare back at him as if he has cast a spell over me. I am waiting for his move. My heart is thumping and I almost can't breathe – and not because he is crushing me with his extremely fit body. Silently, I pray to the love Gods - please kiss me Liam, please kiss me. Then the moment is shattered and Timmy shakes wet sand all over us. Liam springs off me, trying to remove the grains of sand from his eyes.

I scream, 'Timmy, bad dog, how could you?!'

Timmy doesn't seem to care and just rushes back into the sea. Oh, why didn't we just get a cat instead? Timmy has ruined the best moment of my increasingly sad life.

Liam grins and jumps up, pulling me with him. He looks at me and smiles softly.

'I'm sure it's nothing, Annie. There is probably a perfectly good explanation for what you heard this morning. Don't let it get inside your head. As if your sister would do anything like that.'

He takes my hand and I smile at him in relief.

'You're right. I always have jumped to the wrong conclusions on everything. Let's just enjoy our walk and if you're good, we could sneak in a brandy before lunch.'

The trouble is, as we set off after an out-of-control Timmy, I still can't shake the feeling that something is very wrong.

Chapter Thirty

Liam treats me to lunch at the pub. I need to put some distance between myself and my family and he has obviously sensed it.

I enjoy spending time with him. We talk about ourselves, and I think I now know more about his life than anyone I have met in my whole life. I keep on having to remind myself that it's not for much longer. In two days', time we will be packing to head back to London.

I'm sure we'll keep in touch for a bit, until his glamorous life claims him once again.

Liam is also quiet. He seems to have something on his mind and I decide to try to help. After all, isn't that what friends are for?

'Hey, boyfriend. You've gone a bit quiet. Anything you want to share with your temporary girlfriend?'

My heart flutters as he grins that devilish grin that sets my pulse racing and my insides on fire.

'Sorry, I'm just dreading returning to the madness back in London. Being here with you and your family has taught me the importance of family life.'

I look at him incredulously. 'You're joking, aren't you? If I were you, I'd be counting my blessings. At least you get to escape from this madhouse. I must return to it and go through the madness again in a few short months. Who knows what's going on here and things may get a whole lot worse? Just be grateful you have a one-way ticket out of here.'

He smiles sadly. 'I have quite enjoyed the craziness. My life is crazy-free most of the time. My family is so stiff they could have shares in starch. I don't have any brothers or sisters and my only cousin now probably hates me for ruining her wedding. My job, although seemingly glamorous, is lonely and meaningless. I take pictures of empty vessels most of the time. Everything is crafted into an illusion of perfection. What my pictures don't show is the real story. These images are to sell. They are designed to aspire, not inspire. The people I work with are fake and ruthless. I never get to meet real people, Annie, until now that is.'

I shake my head in total surprise. 'But you are so successful, Liam. You have risen to the top of your profession. Now is the time to enjoy that success. You could do so much more if you wanted to. There isn't a law that says you must photograph fashion. Look around you and look for other alternatives. I am sure with your CV you would get most jobs you went for if you tried.'

Liam smiles and then looks at me with interest. 'What about you? If I remember rightly you still need a job.'

I wave my hands dismissively. 'Oh, something will come up. If not, I'll move back home for a bit until I get myself sorted out. It's not the end of the world.'

Taking another sip of the brandy I can't help feeling that if I had to return here, away from my flat, my friends and now Liam, it would very much be the end of my world.

The rest of the afternoon is spent wrapping gifts for the Santa's sack. Liam and I head off to his room for some privacy away from prying eyes.

Mum and Dad have made their Holiday Lets, real homes from home. The rooms are light and airy and have everything a visiting guest would need. No wonder they are always fully booked.

I am quite enjoying myself sitting on the floor of the room with Liam, surrounded by cheap Poundland paper and crazy cheap gifts. As we work we chat about ridiculous things and make each other laugh.

As soon as the last crazy gift is wrapped, I sink back and look at the exciting pile with satisfaction.

'There, all done and dusted. Now we just have it all to look forward to.'

Liam smiles and looks at me strangely. 'You know, Annie, I have had the best time, I really have. When I first saw you on the train, I never imagined we would be sitting here, did you?'

I smile and laugh happily. 'You were so angry that day, as was I. Who'd have thought that a chance meeting would turn out the way it did. We broke every rule out there about what not to do when talking to strangers on the train. For all I knew, you could have been a crazy psycho, whose sole intent was on abducting and murdering me. After a few brandy's though, it ceased to be of any importance.'

Liam grins wickedly. 'And you could have been some mad, crazy, woman, hell bent on seducing me and coercing me into becoming your boyfriend while using me for your own pleasure.'

I snort, feeling my face burn with embarrassment as he grins and pulls me up from the floor.

'Come on, let's give these gifts to your mum and see if we can help with anything else. We have a mystery to solve if I'm not mistaken.'

My eyes must cloud over at the mention of my problems and Liam smiles softly.

'Whatever is going on must have a very simple explanation. If I know one thing, it's your family may be mad, but they're not morally corrupt. Just keep an open mind and the truth will reveal itself.'

I smile at him gratefully. 'You're probably right.'

As we head outside, I pull him back and smile softly.

'Thanks, Liam. I really mean it. This weekend has been kind of crazy and not many men would put up with it. I will miss my crazy boyfriend when we return to normality and the daily grind. I just want you to know that. It's meant a lot.'

Liam's eyes glitter and my breath catches in my throat as he looks at me with such an intense look I almost forget to breathe.

He pulls me towards him and touches my cheek softly. His eyes soften and he smiles gently.

'No, thank you, Annie. As girlfriends go, you are the best one I have ever had. Funny, kind, sweet and sexy. The most beautiful person I have ever met and worth a million supermodels.'

I almost think he is about to kiss me when there is a sharp thump on the door.

'Are you decent in there? Mum wants a hand with stuffing the Turkey and Dad needs a hand splitting logs. The last thing I want, is to spend Christmas Eve with my hand up a Turkey's ass. You'd better come and save me so Dick and I can go to the pub.'

I look at Liam and groan. I now hate my sister. How could she selfishly ruin my finest hour to get herself off the hook? I almost shout back some choice words, but Liam grins.

'Come on, let's go and do our bit.'

As I follow him out, I push down the wanton thoughts of what I would very much rather be.... doing!

Chapter Thirty-One

True to her word, Gina and Dick disappear to the pub with Gran and the Major, leaving Liam and me to do all the work. Liam disappears off outside with my father and I help mum in the kitchen.

Faced with a mountain of Brussels sprouts, I feel like Rapunzel on one of her tasks. Surely there's no need for these many sprouts? Is there even a pan big enough to hold them?

Mum takes on the unenviable task of stuffing the Turkey and dons some plastic surgical gloves for the task ahead.

Christmas carols are playing on the radio and we both have a festive glass of mulled cider to help with even more festive spirit.

Mum spends most of the time singing along to the tunes and soon I join in and just enjoy the moment. This is it, the night before Christmas. Everything is prepped and prepared, in preparation for the perfect Christmas.

The fire is burning and crackling in the grate. Fairy lights twinkle around the cottage, threatening the national grid with overload. Every surface is polished and clean and the cushions are plumped. The gifts look enticing under the tree, guarding their secrets within from prying eyes.

This is my favourite time of all. Mum looks over and smiles happily.

'You know, darling, I love this time the most. All the hard work pays off and we can just relax and enjoy the moment.'

I nod in agreement. 'Yes, mine too. You know, you have worked hard, mum. In fact, you always do. This place looks amazing. I don't know how you do it all, really.'

She laughs happily. 'I love it, you know that. There's not a thing about it that I hate. I take great delight in the preparation; even more so than the actual event itself.'

I hug her warmly. 'I love you, mum. You know, if ever there was anything wrong, you could tell me you know.'

She raises her eyes and laughs. 'Whatever makes you think there's anything wrong, darling. Couldn't be better in fact. Now that you and Gina are settled your father and I have more time for our own hobbies and pastimes. When there are just the two of you, life gets a lot less complicated.'

She turns to the cupboard and pulls out some more vegetables.

'Here you go, Annie, get started on these while I grab the stuff for the table settings. We should have everything done by the time the carol singers arrive.'

I watch her head off into the dining room thoughtfully. She seemed rather hasty to get away and I know my mum. She is hiding something and now I'm very worried.

It must be an hour later that Liam and my Dad come back from log splitting duty. They look frozen and I feel bad for Liam. He must really be regretting his recklessness now. He may even end up with pneumonia for Christmas at this rate.

He smiles that sexy smile of his as he enters the kitchen and I grin at him.

'Come into the warm and I'll make you both a hot chocolate. If you're good I'll even throw in some marshmallows.'

They laugh and my dad sits down at the table and nods to Liam.

'Take a seat son, you've worked hard this afternoon. I must say your prowess with the axe was inspiring.'

Feeling slightly worried about Liam's apparent skill with an axe, I make them both a hot drink.

Mum comes in just as I finish and we all sit together in satisfied exhaustion. I don't miss that this is a perfect opportunity to grill them about what's going on and I look at my father sharply.

'Is everything ok, Dad? I mean, you're not worried about anything, are you?'

He looks surprised and exchanges a look with my mum that I can't explain. He just smiles and shakes his head.

'Everything's fine, poppet. Couldn't be better in fact. Now, what about you two? Got any plans for New Year?'

I look at Liam with exasperation, part of me suitably impressed with my father's avoidance tactics. Liam interrupts.

'Not yet, but I was meaning to ask you, Annie, if you're free to come to a party with me at work.'

My mum looks impressed, and I am filled with complete and utter terror. The last office party I went to didn't go down well at all and the thought of going to such a glamorous one is enough to give me anxiety.

I look at him with surprise as he grins and his eyes twinkle, destroying any defence I may have set in place in an instant. He appears to be taking this pretence into the New Year, despite not having discussed an extension with me first. However, there is a warm feeling spreading through me at the thought of it. It doesn't end here, apparently and now I have something very much to look forward to.

I just nod matter-of-factly. 'Oh, if you like.'

My mum shakes her head. 'Don't sound so enthusiastic, darling. If I was in your shoes, I would be super-excited. Hobnobbing with the rich and famous is not to be dismissed so lightly.'

Liam is struggling to stop laughing and I frown at him.

'Um, Liam, how about we get ready for the carol singers? You can help me light the candles in the driveway and around the tree, if you've warmed up sufficiently.'

Liam grins and my mum nods happily.

'Of course, they'll be here soon. Rose will be back with the boys shortly and we must make sure that everything is in place.'

I look at her with interest. 'Where have they been?'

Dad says. 'Panto in Dorchester. Apparently, there's some character from a programme they love in it that's got them all excited. I think they're having a MacDonald's after, which will make them even more hyper than normal.'

Mum laughs. 'Isn't it lovely to see Christmas through a child's eyes? We must make sure that we put out the brandy and mince pies for Santa, with a carrot for Rudolph. Oh, and Kevin, make sure you cut out a little footprint stencil and sprinkle talcum powder over it to resemble snowy footsteps by the fireplace. I always think it's a magical touch that will stay in their minds forever.'

Liam grins at me and raises his eyes. I know what he's thinking, it won't be Santa swigging that brandy with us around. I just smile at my parents sweetly and head off with Liam outside.

As we set about our task, I quiz Liam on his time with my father.

'Hey, Liam, did you find anything out? Did my father divulge his deep, dark, secret?'

He shakes his head. 'No, just some more strange questions. He tried to pass them off as some friend of his, but I have my doubts.'

My anxiety rushes to the fore and I lower my voice. 'What did he ask you?'

'He said that he was going to ask Dick if bondage was an arrestable offence. Apparently, he thinks it may constitute false imprisonment.'

I feel weak and lean back heavily on a neighbouring tree. 'You are kidding me.'

He shakes his head. 'He also wanted to know if you took photographs of children at a school play and posted them on a web page, could you be arrested for child pornography?'

There is a sudden rush of dizziness to my head and I feel sick. Liam looks at me with concern as I say weakly.

'Ok, Liam, we can't brush all this to one side. These questions are not normal and either my father is into some sick stuff, or my mother is, or both. I don't buy that friends reference either. Dad's only friend is Malcolm Barnaby who he plays darts with.

He is the most unlikely person to do anything other than play with his allotment. I am not leaving until this mystery is solved.'

Liam shifts closer and pulls me towards him whispering, 'Leave it until after Christmas; it's too close now and wouldn't solve anything. Give it a couple more days and then if you still haven't worked it out, I'll back up everything you say. Ok?'

I nod weakly and just sink against his protective body. Thank God, I met Liam on that train. At least I'm not on my own and have him to sound off to.

We are interrupted by a car approaching and look up as the Range Rover skids to a halt in the drive.

The doors fly open and two little tornados rush out, brandishing flickering wands and singing the 'Time Warp,' at the top of their voices. My Aunt follows them looking tired and stressed.

As they dodge in and out of the strategically placed candles and run around the beautifully lit tree, she yells at the top of her voice.

'Fall in soldiers. Santa's watching and wants you both in that house, sitting quietly, while awaiting further orders.'

Immediately, the twins fall into line and march inside. As she looks over my Aunt winks. 'I love Santa. I use him a lot throughout the year. He gets results when all else fails.'

Laughing, we follow her inside.

Chapter Thirty-Two

The others return from the pub in a very merry mood and once again I frown at my sister. Typical, she gets to do all the fun stuff while leaving the work to me. Mind you, I have kind of enjoyed the preparations so far, so I will forgive her this once. What I won't forgive is her cheating on Dick with someone I don't even want to think about.

We all sit around with glasses of wine and the boys have juice. There is great excitement in the air and I laugh as I see the expectation and anticipation on the two little boys' faces.

Elliott grins over at me. 'Not long now, Annie. What do you think Santa will bring you?'

I shake my head. 'Not half as much as he will bring you, I'm sure.'

Barney looks nervous. 'Does he know we're here? Usually he comes to Cornwall. How does he know we aren't there?'

Mum interrupts. 'Because Santa is magic and knows everything. And just in case I emailed him to let him know.'

The boys are suitably impressed at my mum's hotline to Santa and Barney shouts.

'Can I see it, Auntie Sandra? I want to see his email address.'

To her credit, my mum doesn't bat an eyelid. 'Sorry little guy, it self-destructs on send. If everyone knew where to find him, he wouldn't have time to make all those presents, would he?'

Elliott looks thoughtful. 'But don't his elves make the toys? I thought Santa was just a supervisor.'

My aunt laughs and rolls her eyes. 'So many questions guys. Just know that Christmas and Santa is magic. There's no point questioning it because it can't be explained. Anyway, enough questions about Santa because if I'm not mistaken, I can hear bells outside which can only mean one thing.'

We all jump up in excitement. The carollers are here. It's time to crank up the Christmas festivities and what better way than a rousing chorus of, Hark the Herald Angel, followed by, Away in a Manger.

We all rush outside and see the horde of carollers wending their way down the path. They are singing as they go and are a splendid sight to behold.

They are all carrying lanterns with burning candles inside. One man has a guitar and their bright bobble hats dance in time to the music.

Granny claps her hands together in delight. 'Oh, I love a good Christmas carol. Come on Major, let's show them how it's done.'

She drags the Major off to stand by the tree and joins in, singing way too high, not caring how embarrassing it is.

The Major joins in with a deep rousing chorus of, Oh Come all Ye Faithful. I watch Dick grab Gina's hand and pull her against him. She looks up at him with adoration and I sigh inside. Lucky bitch. What I wouldn't give for someone to love me as much as he does her.

Liam grabs my hand and pulls me close to him. Leaning down he whispers. 'Come on, girlfriend, let's get into the party spirit. I bet I can sing louder than you.'

Grinning, I fix him with a determined stare. 'You do know I'll win, don't you?'

He just laughs and we join in with the singing.

Mum appears holding a tray of mince pies and my father follows with a tray of mulled wine.

We all help ourselves and sing our hearts out while warming our cold hands on the mulled nectar. The two boys sing loudly and out of tune which is the most adorable thing I have ever heard. In fact, the complete opposite of how I feel about Granny's singing. Maybe we did get that cat after all.

As we stand here, I feel happier than I have felt in a long time. Liam keeps on shooting me sexy looks and I imagine a time that we are indeed together. How amazing would that be?

It must be a good twenty minutes into the carol extravaganza when I see my Aunt tense up. I follow her gaze and see her looking at one of the singers in disbelief.

Screwing up my eyes to focus in on him, I look behind the Santa's hat and scarf pulled up high around his mouth. In fact, all I can see are his eyes. What is she looking at?

I look between them as they just stare at each other. I can see tears in my Aunt's eyes and look at Liam in shock. Nudging him, I nod towards my Aunt and he looks as mystified as I am.

As the song ends, my mum steps forwards and claps. 'Bravo everyone. You all sang beautifully.'

She turns to the twins and smiles mysteriously. 'Now boys, a little bird told me that you had a special wish this Christmas. Do you want to tell the lovely singers what that was?'

Elliott shifts on his feet and looks furtive. Barney shouts, 'The latest X-Box game. Todd Rivers has it and told me it wasn't available yet. His dad works for the company that makes them and he got one before everyone else. I told him that Santa would bring it if I asked.'

My mum shakes her head, a trifle irritably. 'No, that wasn't it. What else did you wish for?'

Elliott blurts out. 'Bubblehead Barbie.'

I look at Liam and we try not to laugh. My mum looks at him in total astonishment and then recovers well.

'No, there was something else, much more special than that.'

The twins look at each other and then Barney says in a small voice.

'We wanted our daddy home, but mummy said Santa couldn't work miracles.'

My mum laughs with happy relief. 'Then prepare to be amazed, because Santa can do anything, even that. He has delivered you your dearest Christmas wish. Where are you, Steven? You can come out now.'

We all watch in shock as the man in the scarf whips it off and steps forward. He holds out his arms and with an ear-splitting squeal the two boys launch themselves at their father. My Aunt just stands watching, with tears streaming down her cheeks and I don't think there is a dry eye in the garden.

We watch as the father clings to his two little sons and makes their Christmas dreams come true.

Then he pulls back and looks over to his wife. His eyes soften and a lump comes to my throat. He smiles and throws her such a look of love that I feel as if my heart will explode.

'Hello, Rose.'

Just for a minute she stares at him in shock and then they are running towards each other as if they can't get there quickly enough. His arms reach for her and she jumps into them and they cling together.

Suddenly, two little voices ring out in the frosty air. 'Do it! Do it! Do it!'

Liam bursts out laughing and I join him, as I look at the startled expressions around me.

Then, their parents give them what they want and the couple kiss each other as if their lives depended on it.

Then the singing starts again and I laugh when I hear, Halleluiah. Liam and I giggle throughout and then my heart lifts as I see my father with his arm around my mother, laughing at something she is saying. Surely there isn't anything wrong. It must just be my over active imagination.

Once the singing has stopped, we fill their buckets with change and they head off into the night, on to the next house. Mum claps her hands and orders everyone inside.

'Just time for a quick bite to eat before Church. I hope you're all up for midnight Mass tonight.'

As we follow them inside, I take with me a warm feeling inside. This is what it's all about. Being with the people you love and just enjoying the simple things. No presents, no television, and no distractions.

Just good old-fashioned Christmas spirit and I'm so incredibly glad I came.

Chapter Thirty-Three

As it turns out, not many of us make it to the church. After the twins have hung up their stockings they disappear off for a bath and bed. Auntie Rose and Uncle Steven are staying to babysit, amongst other things and Granny and the Major want a game of Bridge instead.

So, just the six of us pile into Kirrin Cars to make the short journey to celebrate the true meaning of Christmas.

I listen to Gina moaning in the back.

'I could so do without this. I'm absolutely knackered and all I want is my bed. After all, who can be bothered to sit in a cold, damp, church, when a warm and cosy bed beckons.'

Mum shakes her head and says irritably.

'Stop moaning, George. You know as well as I do that this is the real reason for celebrating Christmas. It's not all about the presents or eating and drinking until you're sick. There is a specific reason for Christmas and we must celebrate it in the correct manner. Anyway, don't you just love the romance of it all? There is something magical about celebrating Christmas surrounded by candles and singing hymns. It really feeds your soul.'

I grin, as Gina sighs heavily.

'Whatever floats your boat, mum. I notice that gran and the Major managed to dip out. I would have thought they would feel the need to get in a few brownie points with the Almighty more than most.'

I stifle a laugh at my mum's horrified expression.

'Georgina Anderson, I'm ashamed of you. If anyone needs to pray hard this evening it's you, young lady. Maybe you should just look deep inside yourself for the true meaning of Christmas and curb that sharp tongue of yours.'

Liam nudges me and I look out of the window. Gina can't help it. She's always been the same. Where the rest of us just go with the flow, she questions everything. She has never been one to do things she hates. I kind of admire her in a way. She knows what she wants and doesn't let anything stand in her way and to hell with the consequences. Me on the other hand, well, I just do anything to keep the peace. I don't like to rock the boat and just put up with whatever life throws at me.

Maybe I should take a leaf from my sister's book. Of all of us, she appears the happiest and dare I say it, the most normal.

However, as soon as we get to the church, I am pleased that we came.

They have placed little tea lights in jam jars all the way up the path to the entrance. They burn brightly in the dark night and illuminate our journey to enlightenment.

There is a steady stream of worshippers following it and despite the cold, frosty night, I feel warm inside.

Liam takes my hand and smiles happily.

'This is nice, Annie. I haven't been to midnight mass for years. It's certainly a welcome change from the Christmas Eve parties that I normally drag myself to. Hopefully this year I won't wake up with a raging hangover and miss half of the day by laying out cold in bed.'

I nod but feel anxious. I keep on forgetting that Liam is used to living the high life. For some reason, I have forgotten that he is a member of the glitterati and sought after by crazed hormonal women. I wonder why on earth he is here at all? Surely this must all seem boring to him. He should have a supermodel on one arm and a glass of champagne in the other, hobnobbing with the rich and famous. Instead, he is being dragged to our local church with the crazy Famous Five inspired family from Hell. How the mighty have fallen.

When we step inside the doors, I look around me wide-eyed. This is beautiful!

There is a huge Christmas Tree lit with what appears to be real candles. I can't believe they get away with this in the days of health and safety gone mad. Fleetingly, I wonder if this is the start of us taking back control from Brussels. Brexit begins here in a fire hazard in the deepest, darkest, Dorset countryside.

There is festive foliage everywhere and candles are lit on every surface.

Far from feeling cold, there is a warmth inside that reflects in the happy faces around us. I spy a choir at the front all sitting resplendent in their white billowing gowns and hear the gentle tones of the organ playing as we take our seats.

Mum and Dad lead us to a pew about halfway down. The place is filling up fast and there is an expectation in the air. Gina sinks down heavily next to Dick and I watch as they hold hands and sit close together, shutting the rest of us out. Again, I long to be close to someone. How I wish that someone was Liam.

Soon it begins and I thoroughly enjoy myself. I really must get out more if this is my idea of a good time.

I find the whole experience magical. There is something quite calming about singing hymns in the dead of the night, celebrating Christmas with your loved ones. As I sink to my knees on the embroidered kneeler and pray, I offer up a silent prayer to make my Christmas boyfriend last quite a lot further into the new year.

I am woken the next morning by a little hand shaking me. I open one eye and see Elliott peering at me, beaming with excitement.

'Wake up, Annie, Father Christmas has been and mummy says we have to wait until everyone is up before we can open our presents. Hurry up!!'

I smile and want to squeeze him hard. He is so adorable and his excitement is infectious. Then I see the time. 5am!!!

I groan. 'Elliott, it's still night-time, go back to bed.'

His little face falls and I feel bad. Shaking my head, I just grab my dressing gown and grin.

'Come on then. I'll sleep tomorrow. Lead on my friend and let's see if your dreams have come true.'

He giggles excitedly and I laugh as I see Barney pulling a grumpy Gina from her bed.

'Come on Georgie Porgie, you've had enough sleep.'

Gina catches my eye and despite the early hour, grins. Just for a moment, we are transported back to our childhood.

We used to get up even earlier than this and head off to unwrap our presents with great excitement. My dad used to moan but mum always let us. As soon as we had opened them, they went back to bed, leaving Gina and I to play with our toys. By the time they got up we were both exhausted and feeling rather sick, due to the fact that we had eaten every chocolate orange in our stockings.

I say stockings; it was always a pair of dad's socks, stretched to within an inch of their lives. I wonder if people still do that now?

We follow the excited boys, who disappear off quickly to round up the rest. I laugh as I hear a loud voice shouting,

'Bugger off back to bed. Come back when it's 10 am. Some of us need all the sleep we can get.'

Gina grins. 'Typical Gran. I don't think she ever read the manual on the dos and don'ts of raising children. Not swearing in front of children would mean she didn't ever utter one sentence. Isn't it great how the elderly can get away with everything we punish our children for?'

I laugh and sink down onto the settee and wait for the rest. The place looks amazing. Heaps of brightly wrapped parcels lay littered around the fireplace and the tree twinkles merrily in the dark still of the night. 5 am in Winter is still the middle of the night as far as I'm concerned.

We hear the boys excited chatter as they lead two more victims into the room and my heart does a huge somersault as I see Liam walking towards me. Wow, morning Liam is even more gorgeous if that's at all possible. Once again, I want to run my fingers through that hair of his and he wears the designer stubble well. He rakes his hand through his hair and gazes at me sleepily. He has thrown on a pair of tracksuit bottoms and a sweatshirt and if Santa has brought me anything at all it's the sight of him this morning. This image will stay with me forever.

As he looks at me, a grin breaks out across his face and he flops down beside me.

Leaning across, he plants a kiss on my cheek.

'Happy Christmas gorgeous. Sleep well?'

I can feel my heart thumping in my chest as I just manage to squeak out,

'Yes, thank you. What about you?'

He nods. 'Like a log. That is until I was taken prisoner by two relentless warriors.'

I laugh. 'Sorry about that. I'm actually quite impressed they made it to 5 am.'

The door opens and mum comes into the room bearing a tray of tea and coffee.

'Here you go everyone, help yourselves while we wait for the rest.'

It doesn't take the twins long to round up the last few stragglers and then they launch themselves on Santa's gifts like two heat-seeking missiles.

Suddenly, the air is filled with the sounds of tearing paper and cries of joy. Even Timmy gets in on the act and helps scratch the paper from the gifts. All around me are happy faces watching these two little boys have so much fun.

We laugh at the groans as yet another toy is exposed, that will need building or batteries. I know what most of us will be doing this morning.

The best moment is when Elliott unwraps Barbie. Liam nudges me and we watch as he rips the paper off and then squeals in delight.

'I knew he was real. Look, he gave me Bubblehead Barbie, I can't believe it.'

Gina and Dick grin at us and we laugh at the expressions on everyone's faces. My Aunt looks totally bewildered and I hear my uncle whisper, 'Good God, it looks like I returned just in time. What on earth were you thinking?'

My Aunt looks confused and shakes her head. 'I don't know anything about it.'

Gran laughs out loud. 'You're starting young, Elliott. Playing with girls already, you'd better watch him, Rose. It looks like he's taking after my side of the family.'

Liam nudges me and whispers, 'I wonder if his other wish will come true when he returns to school.'

I laugh and then to my surprise he takes my hand in his and squeezes it softly. Leaning down he whispers,

'I love what you did for him, Annie. You're the kindest person I have ever met. I'm glad that we met on the train. This has been the best Christmas of my life so far and it's all thanks to you.'

I blush and strangely feel lost for words. Inside me is a raging torrent of emotions. It feels so good being here with Liam, sharing this family Christmas with him. The trouble is, I must harden my heart because in just a couple of days, we will be back in London and all of this will be forgotten. I'm enough of a realist to know that guys like Liam don't end up with ordinary girls like me. He may be having a good time now but when the mundane takes over, he will be off like a rocket back to Starsville. I must just enjoy this while it lasts.

Chapter Thirty-Four

The rest of the morning is spent trying to remove plastic packaging and building Lego. We must get through two multi-packs of batteries and there is mess everywhere.

Most of the men are enjoying helping the little boys with their toys. Their excitement is contagious and there is lots of excited chatter, drowning out the sound of the Christmas carols that are on a loop on the music channel.

Gina and my Aunt are busy clearing away the packaging while taking crafty sips of Bucks Fizz and chatting about general things. I help my mum with the dinner and Granny and the Major have retreated for a lie-down.

Then the moment we have all been waiting for arrives. Christmas Dinner.

Mum calls us all to sit down and I must admit the table looks amazing. She has excelled herself and her homemade crackers sparkle in the light, nestling beside her beautifully wrapped table presents. The glasses sparkle and the amazing centrepiece of a festive candle ring burns brightly in the middle.

I sit next to Liam and he winks at me. 'I'm so hungry, all that building has made me work up quite an appetite.'

I grin. 'Don't think I didn't see you having way too much fun playing with those presents. In fact, I don't think the twins even got a look in.'

He laughs and my heart tightens. I am going to miss him so much.

Soon we are off and eating the fruits of my mum's hard work. Christmas dinner is like none other. We put so much into it. There is the planning weeks ahead, sometimes months. Recipes are sought out in books and from television programs, all designed to deliver the perfect Christmas meal. The vegetables are grown and frozen under the labels, 'Christmas dinner.' The actual cooking is planned in a military-style operation and the ingredients are sourced from the most reputable providers. All common sense goes out of the window as we indulge in things we would never do normally. The wine is the most expensive we can afford and there are bottles of every kind of drink on earth.

We attend many Christmas fairs in the run-up to the big day. We purchase locally produced wine and alcohol with an Artisan flavour. The desserts are planned and executed with precision and chilled in the mancave when the room in the fridge has been taken. Nothing is left to chance or unplanned and it is all over in well under 30 minutes.

I gaze around me at the devastation. The crackers have been reduced to a pile of packaging, their contents mingling with the crumpled napkins and paper hats. Plates are now dirty and empty and the wine mere dregs at the bottom of the glasses. The candle has dripped wax onto the festive foliage and nearly caused a fire, quickly extinguished by Dick's fast thinking and a nearby glass of water.

Nobody can move and we all just slump back in our seats and pray for a miracle in helping this food digest quickly in readiness for the Christmas pudding and mince pies.

It is at this point that everything goes badly wrong.

As I sink back into my chair, I hear my phone ring. It shatters the peace and everyone looks around thinking it must be theirs. Like everyone, I follow suit and then hear Gran shout.

'Here it is. Good, God!'

We all look at her and she laughs loudly, holding the phone out to me.

'It's for you, Annie darling. It would appear that Tosser has sent you a selfie.'

Feeling my cheeks burn, I grab the phone wildly.

Looking over my shoulder, Gina gasps, 'Oh my God, Annie, is that a dick Pic?!'

All eyes swing to Dick and he holds his hands up. 'Not me.'

Liam snorts, as he looks over my shoulder and tries hard not to laugh.

I can't believe what I am seeing. There, in all its glory, is a picture of Gary's most private part, under the caption.

'*He misses you.*'

Ugh, you have got to be kidding me. My dinner threatens to make an appearance and I look around me shell-shocked.

Mum looks over curiously. 'What's the matter, darling? Don't tell me you also know somebody called Dick and why is he sending you pictures of himself?'

I shake my head, lost for words and say feebly. 'It must be a wrong number.'

Gina snorts and dad looks over at Dick.

'Is there a law against sending people porn pictures without their authorisation? I mean, could they get arrested?'

Gina shouts out angrily. 'Enough dad. What the hell is going on? These questions of yours are getting creepy. Ever since we arrived you've been saying the weirdest things. Something is going on here and I want to know what.'

All eyes swing over to my father who suddenly looks extremely uncomfortable.

'I don't know what you mean.'

I interrupt. 'It's true Dad. These questions are strange. Are you in any trouble because if you are, we can help?'

Dad looks alarmed, for want of a better word and looks at my mum with a panicked expression.

All eyes now turn to her and she rolls her eyes and says angrily.

'I told you not to say anything. You've only got yourself to blame now it's all coming out.'

I look at Liam in shock – Coming Out!! Is this what I think it is?

Liam shakes his head and looks at me with concern as mum sighs heavily.

'Ok, they should know anyway. It's gone on too long and you can't keep it a secret for much longer.'

Gran leans forward and fixes them with an interested look.

'Go on Sandra, you can tell us. I mean, nothing shocks me anymore, isn't that right, Major.'

I feel strangely disturbed to see him wink at her and a little secret smile passes between them. Parking that one for later contemplation, I look over at my mum as she takes my father's hand.

'You should all know that your father has been living as another for some time now.'

I hear Gina's sharp intake of breath as the blood rushes to my head. Liam grabs my hand under the table and squeezes it hard.

Dad looks around the table guiltily. 'I'm afraid it started by accident, really. I was just asked to fill in for someone and then realised I had quite a knack for it. They asked me to carry on and I've been doing it ever since. I wanted to tell you all, but have to keep my identity secret because if anyone found out who I really am then it would be game over.'

Aunt Rose interrupts. 'What are you talking about, Kevin? Should we take the boys outside?'

My mum shakes her head. 'No, it's fine. Just tell them, Kevin, so I can get on with the dessert.'

Clearing his throat, my father stares at us guiltily.

'Well, here goes then. I have been working at the local paper for six months now as an agony aunt. I go by the name, Delilah Dogoody and people send me their problems and I offer advice. It must remain a secret, because if the locals knew it was me then it wouldn't work. Why would they entrust their deepest, darkest, secrets, to someone they know? This way, everyone remains anonymous and I help out where I can.'

The relief is overwhelming. Thank God, an Agony Aunt.

Gina cries, 'What on earth possessed you to call yourself Delilah Dogoody? How lame is that? For god's sake, dad, couldn't you have taken up golf or something?'

Gran just laughs loudly. 'I love it! As soon as dinner is over, take me to your mancave Kevin and let me rifle through your problems. It will keep me going for another twenty years.'

I daren't look at Liam, this is too much. What must he be thinking?

Mum clears her throat. 'Anyway, let's just leave all this and open the Santa's sack in the other room. We can have dessert after the Queen's speech.'

As we follow her from the room, Liam whispers, 'There you go. I told you there would be a rational explanation for his behaviour.'

I shake my head. 'If you think any part of this is rational, then you have been around us for too long already. This isn't normal, Liam. How on earth could you think it is?'

He just laughs and puts his arm around me and pulls me close.

'Come on, girlfriend, I can't wait to see what happens next.'

Chapter Thirty-Five

In our house we have a Santa's sack. The rules are, all gifts must be useful and cost no more than £1.

It's a lucky dip and if you want you can swap with someone else at the end. Everyone throws their gifts into the sack and it's a general free for all.

Mum claps her hands and smiles around the room.

'Right then, Elliott and Barney have kindly offered to play the roles of Santa's elves and will give you all your first gift.'

The boys proceed to race around the room thrusting cheaply wrapped gifts at all and sundry.

I open mine and discover a sponge for the car. Liam has a can of deodorant. Looking over I see the Major pulling a woolly hat down onto his head and I hear Elliott say with surprise, 'Oh, I always wanted one of these.'

As I look over, I laugh out loud at the sight of him brandishing a balloon whisk while pretending it's a sword.

Liam laughs and points to my gran who is holding up a calendar of hunky men triumphantly.

'I'm not swapping these with anyone - got that?'

We all laugh as my uncle holds up a pair of tights. 'Could come in handy for the bank job I will need to carry out to pay my credit cards bills after Christmas.'

My Aunt rolls her eyes and looks at her book on meditation gratefully.

Then we hear Barney cry out in delight. 'Wow, I love these.'

Looking over, we see the slightly disturbing sight of him brandishing a pair of fur wrapped handcuffs. My mum looks utterly surprised as he slaps them on Elliott.

'You're my prisoner and I'm taking you to jail.'

I see my Aunt and Uncle look at each other with incredulous looks and I can feel Liam shaking with laughter beside me.

If only that's where it stopped.

The next round of gifts appears to have come straight from Ann Summers.

Gina holds up a black lacy thong and shouts, 'I never knew they did these in Poundland – gross!'

I look over and immediately wish I hadn't as I see my gran looking at the Major with an extremely suggestive expression, as she rips the head off a marshmallow penis with her teeth. Then I see my mum holding up what appears to be a riding crop in confusion.

'What's going on? Since when did Poundland deal in adult toys?'

My gran laughs loudly. 'They don't. I just thought I'd liven the party up a bit.'

My cheeks flame as Liam holds up a blow-up doll and grins at me.

'A grownups Bubblehead Barbie, if I'm not mistaken.'

My mum, however, is furious.

'I can't believe you mother. What possessed you to buy such filth, at Christmas too. There are children present and a policeman. There must be laws against X-rated gifts before the Queen's speech and if you think I'm bailing you out of jail when you get there, you are very much mistaken.'

Dick bursts out laughing and Gina looks annoyed.

'Leave us out of this. What happened to the giant Toblerone and family pack of nuts that we put in? For god's sake, just move this thing on and then we can get back to the alcohol.'

The boys carry on delivering their parcels, which are opened with a bit more trepidation. Soon we have all amassed a huge pile of useful, cheap, gifts and the swapping begins.

I fight back a smile as Elliott tries to bargain Liam for the blow-up doll in return for the balloon whisk. My Aunt looks horrified and Liam trades him his selection box instead before quickly tucking the doll out of sight under the settee.

Thank goodness the Queen's speech interrupts the proceedings and we get back to the good old-fashioned traditions of Christmas.

After the speech, we once again sit down to another food mountain. This time, there are all sorts of desserts to tempt us. Trifles and profiteroles jostle with the usual Christmas pudding and mince pies. Dad even manages to light the pudding, which is a first, as he always fails miserably at this every other year. Maybe he googled the best practices of igniting your pudding at the same time as he googled Delilah's problems.

After dinner, we all move into the living room to collapse in a heap in front of the television.

Liam sinks down beside me and I lean against him gratefully.

'I'm stuffed. Don't move an inch, you can be my cushion for the rest of the evening.'

He smiles and just pulls me close with his arms wrapped firmly around me. Wow, this is the best and worst Christmas ever.

I must have fallen asleep because I wake up to a familiar sound.

Suddenly, I hear the same moans and groans that woke me up the other day. With a start, I sit up and look around me in confusion. What the Hell! Am I still dreaming?

Suddenly Gina shrieks. 'Oh my God, give me that.'

I watch in shock as she launches herself at Gran who is laughing uncontrollably.

'Thank God, one of the family is doing me proud. Well done Gina, I'm so proud of you.'

I watch, as Gina grabs what appears to be her iPad, off a howling grandmother, as the rest of the room look at them in stunned silence.

Dick looks mightily uncomfortable as my mum says loudly.

'What's going on?'

Gran wipes her eyes and waves her hand in my direction. 'Annie's dick pick is nothing compared to Gina's porno.'

There is silence in the room and then my Aunt says loudly.

'Come on boys, let's take Timmy for a walk on the beach and you can try out those kites that Santa made for you.'

They rush out of the room leaving the rest of us looking at Gina in disbelief.

She just shrugs. 'So what, it's nothing these days.'

My mum says faintly. 'What are you talking about? That isn't really you, is it?'

Gina snaps the lid closed and looks at Dick and shrugs.

'Listen, you may as well know the truth. Dick and I want to move in together and buy our own place.

As you know, property prices are through the roof and we need a hefty deposit. Well, Dick knows someone who could post this for us on the dark web. It's all perfectly fine because I have been editing it to cut out our faces. Nobody will know it's us and his friend says that we could have our deposit in record time if we just set up a pay to view. See, nothing bad. If it's good enough for celebrities, then it's good enough for us. Everyone does it now.'

All eyes turn to Liam and me and I turn as red as Santa's suit.

'Don't look at us. We aren't in the porn movie business.'

My mum sinks down heavily. 'I can't believe it. I would never have thought it of you, Gina, or you, Dick. Isn't it against the law? You could be arrested.'

Gina shrieks. 'Oh, don't you start. I told you, nobody will ever know. It's not on Google for god's sake, unlike Delilah over there. This is a means to an end and nobody will ever know.'

She looks at Dick and nods towards the door. 'Come on, I need some fresh air. The stench of puritanical judgement and misunderstanding is stifling me. Let's catch the others up.'

Dick looks around apologetically and follows her from the room.

Mum looks extremely shaken up and I feel bad for her. She looks at the rest of us and says quietly.

'Anyone else got anything they want to share?'

We shake our heads, but then Gran pipes up. 'Well, you may as well know that the Major and I have fallen in love and will be getting married in the New Year. Gina isn't the only one who has been having sexy fun this Christmas. He has agreed to move in with me to the McCarthy Stone residence, immediately.'

There is a stunned silence, broken only by my mother reaching for the brandy bottle.

'Pour me a large one, Kevin. God knows I need it.'

Chapter Thirty-Six

Liam and I made a hasty exit back to his room to get over the shock. I think this is now possibly my worst Christmas ever. God only knows what he must think of us.

We sit on his bed and he just holds me and says softly.

'Well, you must be relieved that it's all over and everything's out in the open.'

I look at him in surprise. 'Not really. I mean, it's bad enough finding your dad is some sort of female agony aunt, with the most ridiculous name I have ever heard. If it ever got out, he would be ostracised from not only the darts club but the whole of society.

My sister, as it turns out, is now a fledgling porn star, selling sex for a deposit on a house. Possibly the worse thing of all is even my Gran is having a sex life and has found true lust again, when I, yet again, have not. I have a pretend boyfriend because my real one decided to cheat on me in front of the whole of London and I lost my job and soon my home. In a couple of days, I will have to return to the mess I have created and sort it out. Then I will lose the one person who has got me through all of this and the only one I can tell anything to.'

The tears run down my cheeks as Liam holds me and strokes my hair.

As I well and truly lose it and my mascara runs all over his nice white shirt, his phone rings.

Sniffing, I pull back and nod towards it. 'Go on, Liam, answer that, I'll just clean myself up in your bathroom if I may.'

He smiles, which makes my heart flutter and reaches for his phone. As I close the bathroom door, I hear him say softly, *'Thank god you've called.'*

Ok, I know I shouldn't and there is probably a law against listening to someone's conversation without them knowing, but I am temporarily insane.

Leaving the door slightly ajar, I stand behind it and listen. I hear Liam's low, husky, tones and strain to hear what's he saying.

'No, I'm sorry baby girl..... Yes, it was all a misunderstanding. I'm sure we can work it all out.... Don't cry we'll sort it.... Yes, I know it couldn't have happened at a worse time.... Oh, she won't mind...... (groans) me too.... remember I love

you…… I'll get there as soon as I can……. Ok, beautiful…… Love you.'

He hangs up and I feel my legs shaking. That's it, my bubble has burst. Even my pretend boyfriend has woken up and is heading back to reality.

As I stare at my reflection in the mirror, I don't like what is staring back at me.

Annie Anderson, Famous Five reject and lonely girl. Nothing to look forward to and facing an uncertain future. About to lose the best boyfriend she has ever had after possibly the worst Christmas ever.

As I stare at myself, something stirs within me. This is it, rock bottom. Now the only way is up and I am going to claw my way back up there with courage and determination. I won't let myself be beaten.

Plastering a smile on my face, I head back into the room. Liam jumps up looking apologetic and nods towards the phone.

'Listen, Annie, something's come up and I have to go back to the wedding. I would ask you to come but it would probably be better if you stayed and sorted things out with your family. Do you mind? I hate leaving you.'

He is looking at me with so much concern that my resolve is in danger of crumbling. I just smile weakly and shake my head. 'No, it's fine. You must do what you have to. Don't worry about me, I'll be ok.'

He looks at me anxiously. 'Are you sure? I hate leaving you amid all this chaos.'

I laugh a bit too loudly and note the surprise in his eyes.

'Oh, this is nothing. We'll be back to normal in no time. Do you need a lift to the hotel? I don't think my dad had much to drink, he'll drop you there.'

Liam looks at me strangely and then crosses the room. He pulls me towards him and hugs me tightly.

'Thank you for the best Christmas I have ever had, so far anyway. I'll deal with the drama and get back as quickly as possible. I promise.'

I just smile, trying to muster every last shred of dignity that I have left and say brightly.

'Listen, sort things out there first. After all, we were due to leave the day after tomorrow anyway. If you can make it back then great if not then no biggie. Don't feel as if you should. Anyway, I'll go and get dad to fire up the Kirrin wagon while you pack.'

I turn to go, but he grabs my hand and says softly.

'You know, you're the best pretend girlfriend I have ever had.'

I smile shakily. 'Same goes for me, boyfriend. I'll certainly never forget this Christmas.'

He nods, but his eyes cloud over and suddenly he looks unsure of himself.

'Remember, Annie, if I don't make it back you have agreed to be my date for New Year.'

I smile and nod. 'That's fine. Of course, I'll help you out, it's the least I can do. Anyway, you had better pack and I'll organise your transport.'

As I walk away, I leave my heart in his room. Why did that just feel like we said goodbye?

Chapter Thirty-Seven

Boxing day comes and I wake up with a heavy heart. As I look over at Mr Puddles, it all comes rushing back.

Liam left, and I absolutely drenched Mr Puddles. I really should get him dry-cleaned. I mean, the number of bacteria he must now be holding is surely a public health hazard.

My family were surprised and disappointed that Liam had to leave, but not nearly as much as I was.

Gina and Dick returned and brazened it out. There was an awkward silence in the room, and only gran and the Major seemed in high spirits.

I managed to escape for an early night and must have fallen asleep after crying into Mr Puddles for close on two hours.

I get dressed and venture downstairs. Gina appears to have slept in Dick's room last night. I suppose there was no point in segregating them after the sex scandal and once again I feel jealous of her happiness.

Mum looks up as I enter the kitchen and smiles. However, I note the worry in her eyes and instantly feel bad for her ruined Christmas.

'Morning darling, did you sleep well? That was certainly an eventful day yesterday.'

I go over and hug her, saying softly. 'Let me make breakfast today, mum. You look as if you could use some tlc today.'

She just laughs softly and waves her hands around.

'Don't be silly my dear. I need the distraction quite frankly. It would appear I must organise a geriatric wedding for early spring. That doesn't give me much time to plan, so it will be all systems go as soon as the last mince pie is eaten.'

She pours me a cup of tea and I sit and wait for the others to join us.

Breakfast is a slightly subdued affair and only the twins appear in high spirits. I volunteer to take them for a walk on the beach and we set off on a bracing adventure.

I watch as they run and jump the waves and remember the last time we did this. I wonder what Liam is doing now? Is he even thinking of me at all, or am I just a bad memory already?

Timmy races back and shakes his wet fur over me. Elliott follows laughing.

'Where's Liam? He was fun why did he have to go?'

I just smile. 'He had to return to his family. He may be back later though.'

Elliott cheers. 'I hope so, I want to see if he still has that doll. I could swap with him. Maybe Macie Green would prefer that one instead.'

Despite my feelings, I just laugh out loud. 'I doubt it, darling, I think Barbie is a safer bet.'

Pushing my desolation to one side I decided to just run and be free with the twins. We spend a good hour on the beach, flying the kite and jumping the waves. It's time to forget my troubles and just be a kid again.

When we get back the others are all watching television in the living room.

I join them while mum heads off to make us all a hot chocolate.

Then suddenly, my world turns upside down – again!

The local news comes on and I am faced with the sight of a reporter, standing outside Kingsley Manor.

Earlier yesterday, April Loveday, flew into town in a helicopter, landing here at Kingsley Manor. The Supermodel appears to be attending the wedding of her boyfriend's cousin, who she was rumoured to have split from.

My heart lurches, as we see pictures of April, looking unbelievably beautiful in her Chanel campaign, flashing up on the screen.

Gina sighs. 'God, I wish I looked like that. Some girls have everything, lucky bitch.'

I can feel my world shattering as another image of her with Liam, flashes on the screen.

Seen here with Liam Goodwin, her boyfriend, and top photographer, it is thought they had split. However, a source close to the couple brushed off the rumours and confirmed they are very much back together and spent Christmas evening holed up in their suite. A statement released earlier this morning confirmed that the couple were working things out and were just happy to be together at Christmas.

There is silence in the room and mum comes in, just as the picture of Liam and April flicks onto the screen. She exclaims.

'Good god, is that Julian with April Loveday? If not, he must have a twin.'

All eyes turn to me and I shrink back into my chair, saying weakly.

'Now I'm afraid it's my turn to come clean.'

They look at me expectantly as the TV changes to adverts and I sigh heavily.

'I'm sorry everyone, but Julian is actually called Liam Goodwin. I met him on the train coming down and agreed to be his girlfriend for Christmas. It's true, he is April's boyfriend, but they had split up before I met him. I went to his family wedding, and he came here. It looks like he is back with April though, so at least he had a happy ending out of all this.'

My mum sinks down next to me and looks incredulous.

'Why Anne? It all seems so strange. Why would you want to pretend you had a boyfriend? Also, why would you pick up a stranger from the train and put yourself in danger like that?'

My Dad looks at me with concern.

'Yes, why Anne? You are usually such a sensible girl.'

Gran just laughs loudly. 'Well, I think it's hilarious. Definitely something I would do. Shame you didn't get to do more than pretend. If he had been my boyfriend for even five minutes, I would have been giving him everything he wanted, and more.'

Everyone turns to my gran and shouts.

'Shut up Gran.'

She looks offended and barks angrily. 'Don't call me that. My name is Lizzie and you would do well to remember.'

She looks over at the Major and says irritably.

'Come on dear, you can take me for a walk around the garden, while we leave the rest of them to dwell on how they speak to their elders and betters.'

They storm out of the room and my Uncle Steven looks at me kindly.

'I'm sorry, Annie. I'll take the boys to our room and set up the new model railway. Give you a bit of privacy.'

My Aunt hugs me gently and whispers, 'I'd better go and help. By the time he's laid out all the pieces and read through the instructions, it will be New Year. I'll have it built by the time he's put his reading glasses on.'

The remaining five of us sit and stare at each other and I just shrug.

'I'm sorry, guys. I thought it would be a good idea. I liked Liam and we sort of just clicked. My real boyfriend, aka Tosser, cheated on me at his office party with some tart in the stationery cupboard. Earlier that day I had been relieved of my job so when I met Liam, I was jobless, loveless and heading home to tell you all the bad news. I suppose I was reckless, but it seemed like a good idea at the time.'

My mum just puts her arm around me and my dad comes and does the same the other side.

'Don't worry, Anne. You can always come home and live with us.'

I look at Gina and see the horror in my eyes reflected in hers. She looks at me with a surprisingly uncharacteristic soft expression.

'I'm sorry, Annie. If it's any consolation, I think Liam really did like you.'

I shake my head and laugh ruefully.

'Maybe as friends, but how could I ever compete for someone like him with April Loveday waiting on the side-lines.'

Dick looks thoughtful. 'It doesn't add up. I mean, I'm a guy and I know how we think. Liam talked of nothing else but you in every conversation we had. I just know he liked you, he's not that good an actor, surely?'

Gina nods. 'It's true. I saw the way he looked at you when he thought nobody was looking. That guy had it bad, and I just thought it was because you were in the first flush of love. He couldn't fake that, fake boyfriend or not.'

I stare at them all angrily. 'Well he doesn't, didn't or whatever else you think. Liam has gone now and was never my boyfriend. I will head home tomorrow and try to put my life back together. I may see him again as friends, but doubt it now he's back with April. I'm sorry we deceived you, but there it is. Now we all had secrets to reveal so can no longer judge each other. Let's just enjoy what time we have left and sweep this all under the settee with that blow-up doll of Liam's.'

Reaching down, I search for the doll, to wave her to the room in a dramatic fashion to emphasise my point. However, all I find is a discarded sweet wrapper.

Looking around me wildly, I gasp, 'Oh my god, who's taken blow-up Barbie?'

Chapter Thirty-Eight

Liam never came back and so here I am heading home on the train with only my cracker brandy for company.

I lean my head against the window and stare morosely at the scenery flashing by in a blur.

He never called and with every hour that passed the realisation set in – he isn't coming back; the dream has ended.

When I get back to my flat, it seems cold and empty - much like my heart and I sink down onto the settee, putting my head in my hands.

Christmas is over and in the cold light of day my troubles are racing back with a vengeance.

With a heavy heart, I flick on my answerphone.

The first voice I hear is Tosser. Typical!

Please answer baby, I'm so sorry. I was drunk, and it meant nothing. You are the one I love, please call me and let me make it up to you.

There are fifteen more after that, all along the same lines. It's funny, but I appear emotionally detached from him now. He has ceased to hold any importance in my life and I feel quite shocked about that. The trouble is, I think Liam has ruined all other men for me forever. How on earth could anyone ever compare to him?

The machine beeps again and I hear Gail's voice, sounding strangely hesitant.

Um, call me when you get this Annie. I may have some good news for you. I hope you had a good Christmas.

Strange, she didn't sound herself at all.

Immediately, I reach for the phone and dial her number. She answers quickly and unusually for her, sounds reserved.

'Hi, Annie, did you have a good Christmas?'

I sigh heavily. 'As good as it could be given the circumstances. What about you? Did you go home to your parents?'

She laughs nervously. 'Um, no, I had a slight change of plans at the last minute. Listen, can you meet me at Gio's? There are two things I need to tell you.'

My curiosity gets the better of me. 'Ok, what time suits you? It will take me 30 minutes if you want to meet up now.'

She laughs nervously. 'Great, see you in thirty then.'

As she rings off, I know she's hiding something. Gail is the loudest, most vivacious girl I know and usually shouts on the phone. Today she appeared quiet and reserved. I hope she hasn't lost her job as well? Something's up and a feeling of dread comes over me. Just the tone of her voice tells me that whatever it is, I'm not going to like one bit.

Thirty minutes later I push my way into Giovanni's and look around me furtively. I hope, other than Gail, I don't see anyone I know. I've got rather a lot of fences to mend and if I see anyone from work or Tosser, then I'm walking straight out.

By the time I grab myself a tea – I can no longer stretch to a coffee – Gail rushes through the door, looking around her wildly.

As she sees me, a flicker of trepidation passes across her face and then she smiles and races over for a hug.

'I've missed you, babe. It's not been the same here without you.'

I laugh and push her away. 'I've only been gone a few days. Anyway, the curiosity is killing me. What's the big news?'

Suddenly, her face flushes and she looks uneasy. Grabbing my arm, she steers me to a booth in the corner, shouting her order over to the Barista.

She stares at me long and hard and then looks almost apologetic.

'Listen, Annie. I've got good news and bad news. I'm not sure what you're going to think, so I'll tell you the good news first and then you may not hate me quite so much.'

I shake my head in confusion. 'You're talking in riddles, Gail, just spit it out, I won't mind whatever it is.'

The waiter brings the drinks over and she takes a deep breath.

'Well, I have been asking around regarding jobs for you. I asked everyone that came to the salon and as it happens one of them came up trumps.'

I lean forward, suddenly very interested. 'What is it?'

She smiles happily. 'One of my regulars works at Harris and Goldstein, you know, the Investment bank. Rebecca is Head of Acquisitions and Mergers and we got talking. When I told her what happened to you she got angry. Apparently, they did the same thing to a friend of hers and she was more than angry on your behalf. She can't stand your old bosses and ranted on about them for quite some time. Well, to cut a long story short, she gave me her card and told me to tell you to call her after Christmas. They have a few openings for accountants and she's confident that she will be able to throw one of them your way.'

I can't believe it. Harris and Goldstein are huge. Majorly corporate and occupying the flashiest offices in town. Wow and double Wow!

I jump up and hug her, yelling, 'Thank you! Thank you! I can't believe it. Are you sure though? I mean, do you really think she has a job for me there?'

Gail grins. 'Sure thing. She told me that she couldn't wait to meet you as you would have a lot in common already. Give her a call, or email her if you prefer. There's no time like the present and you may as well get in just after the New Year.'

I slump back in my chair, smiling broadly.

Then Gail's expression changes, and she looks worried.

'Um, now for the bad news.'

Something about the way she is looking so guiltily at me sets off the warning sirens in my head. I know that look. Whatever is bothering her concerns me. What has she done?

I look at her sharply and she sighs heavily.

'Listen, Annie, I just want to say that I didn't mean for it to happen. If anything, I am more surprised about it than you. Neither of us wanted to hurt you, but events kind of got in the way and now there is no turning back.'

An icy hand grips my heart and I feel my world spinning around me. Oh no! This had better not be what I think it is.

I shake my head and whisper, 'Please don't tell me you're now with Tosser? I don't think I could bear it.'

Gail laughs and rolls her eyes in disbelief. 'As if, credit me with some taste after what he did to you.'

I look at her in confusion.

'What then? Oh no, you didn't set me up with someone – please say you didn't.'

Shaking her head, she smiles nervously. 'I'm sorry, Annie, I know you like him, but I am now sort of going out with Alex.'

Just for a moment, I can't think who Alex is. I narrow my eyes and try to picture him. Then I remember – Tosser's boss from the Insurance company.

As she sees the penny drop, Gail blushes and looks worried. I just start laughing, more with relief than anything, and look at her with interest.

'Why should I mind about that? He was nice, you're amazing, why shouldn't you get together. But how did it happen?'

The relief on Gail's face is tremendous, and she smiles broadly.

'Well, after you left, I decided to go and confront Tosser. I wanted to give him a piece of my mind, so I headed in there one lunchtime. After I let him have it in front of his whole office, Alex appeared and escorted me out.

As it turned out he thought the whole thing hysterical and offered to buy me lunch. He said that what Gary did was despicable, and he had felt sorry for you. Well, we got talking and got on like a house on fire. We have loads in common and not just our hatred for a certain ex-boyfriend of yours. To cut a long story short, he asked me out on a date and we have been inseparable ever since.'

Seeing her happy face makes me happier than I have felt since Liam left. Reaching over I squeeze her hand.

'How could I be angry? I'm really pleased for you both. I'm glad at least one of us has found love.'

Gail grins, then her eyes cloud over. 'What happened with that sexy stranger you sent me the picture of?'

I feel my face fall and she looks at me with concern. I shrug and try to gloss over it.

'Oh him. It was nothing. Just a guy I met on the train. We had a laugh for a bit and then he headed back to his girlfriend.'

She looks concerned – damn, she knows me so well. The trouble is, I'm not ready to talk about Liam yet, maybe I never will be.

Chapter Thirty-Nine

For the next few days, I hide out in my flat. Gail tried to get me to go to Divas with her and Alex but I resisted, inventing some Christmas illness that I picked up in Dorset.

The one positive thing I do is email Gail's customer about the job. Almost immediately she replied with a date for an Interview on the 2nd of January. At least I have one thing to look forward to.

Instead, I just veg out on the couch eating junk food and watching Christmas films. Many a tear is shed over these movies, even the funny ones. I am obviously in an extremely fragile mental state.

I hear my neighbour upstairs going at it with her latest boyfriend. I have labelled her, *'Debbie does Dallas,'* because she appears to have a different boyfriend every week. I've seen them come and go and only bodybuilders with tattoos need apply. Lucky bitch!

The sound of the banging on the ceiling is barely drowned out by the television. At least someone is having sexy fun this Christmas, other than my gran.

Pushing the disturbing thought from my mind, I reach for the family tub of ice-cream that came with my bargain bucket from KFC.

Before I've even eaten my second spoonful, the doorbell rings. That's odd, who on earth could be calling? I don't know anyone around here. Maybe they need to read the gas meter.

I flop over to the door and blink in surprise as Gina bowls into the room, closely followed by Dick.

'What?! What are you doing here?'

Gina wrinkles up her nose in disgust as she takes in the sight of the discarded takeout cartons and blaring television. Shaking her head in disapproval, she locates the remote and turns the television off. The sounds of Debbie going at it upstairs fill the room and Gina looks at me in surprise.

'Good God, is that what I think it is?'

I giggle at the disapproval on her face and can't help retorting, 'Well, you should know.'

Dick snorts and rather skilfully turns it into a cough as Gina looks daggers at me.

'What's going on Annie? This place is a pigsty. Is this how you live?'

Sinking down onto the settee, I just shake my head sadly.

'Now it is. It's the only bit of comfort I have as my life has somehow imploded of late and my prospects fell to zero.'

Gina looks at Dick and I almost see a little compassion flash across her face, then it is gone and replaced by the no-nonsense sister that I know and love.

'Right then, Annie, we have come here to save you from yourself. It's New Year's Eve and we have a party to go to.'

I open my mouth to object and she silences me with her ninja stare.

'Come on, go and put on that red dress of yours. Don't worry about hair and makeup, we've got that covered. While we wait, Dick and I will try to bring some order to this chaotic place.'

She holds her hand up to silence the objection forming on my lips.

'Non-negotiable I'm afraid. Now hurry, before I send Dick up to arrest your neighbour for breach of the peace.'

She looks around, shaking her head.

'I've seen crime scenes tidier than this place. I must say, I'm surprised at the extent you have let yourself go. I mean, this isn't like you. You've always been the homemaker after all.'

Dick laughs, as I chuck every cushion I own at her. Gina laughs and her eyes soften.

'That's better. Now, let's show London how the Anderson's party.'

As I sit in the back of Dick's battered Volvo, I almost feel as if I've been kidnapped. I must say, I look and feel a right mess. I wonder what Gina has up her sleeve?

It must take us forty minutes before Dick pulls into a vacant spot on a side road just off Hanover Square. There are hordes of people milling around and I'm surprised we found a space.

I wonder if they have tickets to the fireworks. I love London at night and despite the cold, it's a warm and fun place to be. The lights light up the ancient buildings and bathe them in a fascinating light. Everything looks exciting at night, disguising the rather shabby streets and dusty pavements.

Gina grabs my hand and then looks at me with excitement in her eyes.

'Come on, let's go and have the night of our lives.'

Dick grins and I look at them in surprise.

'Why, what have you got planned?'

Gina just smiles secretively. 'You'll see.'

I follow them to a beautiful Regency building. As we turn the corner, my heart stops and panic fills my soul. Oh no, surely not.

My heart beats wildly as I look up at the words above the door. '*Vogue House.*'

Before I can object, Gina grabs my hand and pulls me forcibly inside. Dick brings up the rear and I realise that escape is not an option. I have been well and truly stitched up and I look a complete and utter mess.

As we get inside an extremely smart and stylish woman sashays across the lobby with a large smile on her face.

'Hi, you must be Liam's friends.'

I feel sick and need to lie down. How could she bring me here?

Gina smiles, and the lady extends her hand.

'I'm pleased to meet you all. If you'll come this way, we're ready for you.'

Gina's eyes flash with excitement and she grins at me. 'Oh, my God. I can't believe we're doing this.'

Shaking my head, I whisper angrily. 'Doing what? Please don't say you've brought me to Liam's party. If you have, I'll never forgive you.'

She just shrugs her shoulders and flashes Dick an excited look as we follow the perfect woman into the lift.

I can't seem to calm the butterflies leaping around inside me. The thought of seeing Liam is overwhelming. The fact that he is probably here with April is just the icing on the cake. Looking like I do now will just emphasise the fact that he had a lucky escape. Not that we ever were a couple, but we were in my dreams.

The perfect girl smiles at us, and even her smile is perfect. I must get some veneers just as soon as they offer them on the National Health Service. I want a million-dollar smile even if my bank account is empty.

Looking around me, I see how the other half live. Liam's place is chic and cool and we have absolutely no business whatsoever being here.

She stops outside a door at the end of the hallway and knocks sharply. As she opens it, she says loudly, 'They're here.'

I follow Gina into the room and blink in disbelief.

We appear to be in a room filled with makeup. There are huge mirrors on the wall and seats placed in front of them facing every known makeup product ever made. Another pretty girl with pink hair smiles and bounds towards us like an exuberant puppy.

'Hi guys, glad you made it. Which one is Annie?'

Gina points to me and she laughs and grabs my arm.

'Oh, this should be easy. Come this way Annie, you are about to be transformed.'

I notice the other perfect lady nods to Gina and we follow them to a couple of chairs set before two sinks. My captor smiles a brilliant white smile and thrusts a gown at me.

'Right, put this on so we don't ruin your lovely dress. I am now your fairy godmother and you are about to have the supermodel treatment. By the time I finish with you, there won't be a woman in town that will outshine you this evening.'

Gina laughs happily and Dick sinks down heavily on a nearby couch and grabs a magazine, already looking bored out of his mind. I actually can't speak. Am I dreaming? What the hell is going on?

What happens next beggar's belief. Abby, my pink-haired fairy godmother, proceeds to transform me right before my eyes.

She chatters incessantly as she works and tells us many stories about the famous people who have sat where we are now. Slowly but surely, I am transformed.

She washes my hair and then wraps it up into large Velcro rollers.

Then she sets to work on my face and totally transforms me. The person I see in the mirror is a total imposter. Annie Anderson may have entered the building, but she is no longer present. The person staring back at me is beautiful. Abby certainly knows her stuff because I simply don't recognise myself.

Gina has also been similarly transformed and I giggle as I see Dick's incredulous expression.

All the time they work we all sip Champagne from a huge bottle sitting on the nearby worktop. The sound of laughter fills the room and I hope this isn't a dream because if it is I never want to wake up.

Finally, she whips off my protective robe and spins my chair around with a flourish.

'There you go, Annie, meet the newest Supermodel in town.'

As I see myself staring back at me, my eyes fill up and Abby looks at me with alarm.

'Save your tears honey, they will ruin my creation.'

I look at Gina and do a double take. Wow! she looks amazing. Her eyes sparkle happily and she grins.

'Well, Annie, what do you think?'

Everyone looks at me expectantly and I shake my head in disbelief.

'I can't believe it. You're amazing Abby. This isn't me where have I gone?'

Abby and her friend, who I now know to be called Poppy, grin at each other and high five.

'Good job girlfriend. Now for the tickets to the ball.'

They smile at us and say excitedly.

'Right, the party is three floors up. It's just the staff and a few guests, nothing to worry about. Just remember to have fun and don't worry about a thing. If you need anything just come and find us. Although don't leave it too long, Poppy and I are usually out of it by 11 pm.'

They laugh and head towards the door. 'Come on, we'll walk with you.'

My heart is pounding as I follow them from the room. Despite looking the best I have ever looked in my whole life, I feel sick with nerves. I don't think I can do this. Seeing Liam with April will just finish me off.

We walk silently towards the lift and all crowd inside.

I watch a look pass between the two girls and wonder what it means. They look excited and a little secretive.

The lift stops and Abby takes my hand and pulls me from the lift, telling the others, 'We're getting off here. Poppy will take you both up to the party.

My instructions are to take Annie somewhere else first.'

I look at Gina and Dick in alarm, but they just grin knowingly as the lift doors close.

Abby grins and winks at me and I follow her down the hallway. Now I know I'm going to be sick.

Chapter Forty

Abby stops outside a door and grins at me.

'Here you go, Annie. Liam asked that you meet him here.'

She looks around and then leans forward whispering, 'You do know he's a great guy, don't you?'

I nod and she laughs softly. 'He's a favourite around here, most of us would do anything for him. We want him to be happy and so agreed to help.'

She winks and heads off before I can ask – help with what?

Feeling extremely nervous, I push open the door.

It appears to be a smallish room which is bathed in subdued lighting. It takes a moment for my eyes to adjust as I look around. The room is empty and there is no sign of Liam.

However, as I look around me, I suddenly focus on something that completely blows my mind. What the hell?!!!

All around me are photographs. It's like some crazy stalker wall, as plastered on every bit of space is me.

Photos and photos of me, cataloguing every minute of my time with Liam. I shake my head and move closer. I can't believe it. These photos are gorgeous. I can't believe it's me. The person on the wall is beautiful. Liam has captured every expression; every laugh and pure emotion and I have never looked so good. Wow, he is a master at this. Who knew he could work such miracles?

Suddenly I hear, 'What do you think, gorgeous?'

Spinning around, my breath leaves my body, as I see Liam in all his sexy glory, leaning nonchalantly against the wall watching me. He looks super-hot, wearing a black tuxedo which makes him look just like James Bond. My legs feel weak with longing and my heart flutters at the sight of him. It's not fair, how can one person be given so much sex appeal?

He looks at me nervously and I remember that he asked me a question.

I just look at him, totally gob-smacked, for want of a better word.

'I can't believe it; these photographs are beautiful. Did you photoshop them or something?'

Liam laughs and comes and stands beside me.

'No, I just captured the moment. I don't think you realise just how beautiful you are, Annie. These photos needed no work. The subject was more than good enough. The camera appears to love you.'

I shake my head and carry on looking at them. 'But why Liam? I never even saw you take these.'

He laughs softly. 'It was easy. Every time I took photos of the happy couple, I took some of you at the same time. You were a much more interesting subject, and I got a bit carried away.'

I look at him in disbelief. 'But why all this? I mean, it smacks of some kind of crazy stalkerish behaviour if I'm perfectly honest. It's a good job I have been accompanied here by the Police.'

I grin and he laughs softly. 'There's my girl.'

Something about the way he says it makes my heart lift. He is looking at me with a strange expression and I feel suddenly nervous.

'Um, this is all lovely and totally unexpected, but why? Surely you have better things to do now that you're back with April. I know you asked me to be your date for this party, but I didn't think the invitation still stood after your reconciliation.'

Liam suddenly looks angry and takes my hand and looks deeply into my eyes.

'There never was a reconciliation, Annie. Despite my mother's best attempts. I think I should start at the beginning, don't you?'

He leads me over to a couch and pulls me down beside him. I do notice that he keeps his hand in mine which feels nice. He looks nervous again, so I squeeze his hand.

'Go on then?'

He smiles softly. 'When I left you, I headed back to the wedding. My cousin Charlotte called – you remember, you were there at the time.'

Gosh, the relief is overwhelming. Charlotte!!

He carries on. 'Well, unfortunately, their wedding night didn't quite go as planned. Eric got raging drunk and collapsed in the bar. Charlotte spent her wedding night alone while he slept it off. If only that was the worst thing that happened. The next day he recovered, and they tried to start again. That afternoon though he disappeared and when she went to find him, she discovered him with one of her bridesmaids in their honeymoon suite. She was meant to be enjoying the use of the spa at the time so he thought he would be perfectly safe. Well, things went from bad to worse and they had a screaming fight. It ended up with her father punching Eric and throwing him out. She called me in floods of tears and asked if I would go back for moral support in case he came back. She was worried they had judged you harshly, and that you hated them all.'

I can't believe what I'm hearing. Poor Charlotte.

'So why did the news channel report that you were back with April? Where does she come into all this?'

He shakes his head. 'My mother called her when she knew I was coming back and said that I was regretting ending it. She told her to get back to the wedding and fight for me. April, meanwhile, discovered she was better off with me as her fling had gone back to his wife. She came to claim her man, and I wanted none of it. I think she spent the night in our old room while I kept Charlotte company in hers.'

I can't take it all in and just look at him in shock.

'Wow, I mean, as wedding's go, that one will keep the staff talking for months.'

Liam laughs and then looks worried again. 'I tried to call you. I wanted to come back so badly but couldn't leave Charlotte. The trouble is, you never picked up, and I left you so many voice messages I thought you had replaced my number with Tosser's.'

I look at him in shock. 'You never called me and come to think of it, I don't think I even had your number.'

Liam suddenly laughs and rolls his eyes. 'It appears that was one small detail we both overlooked. When I realised I hadn't taken your number, I remembered you had given your business card to Aunt Kim. Luckily, she still had it, so I used the number on there.'

I am still confused. 'But there weren't any missed calls or voicemail messages.'

Liam suddenly laughs and his eyes crinkle up at the corners that always makes me go weak at the knees.

'Like I said, I thought you were ignoring them until I got a call from an irate truck driver called Mickey from South Shields. He threatened to come and thump my gay ass if I pestered him anymore. His girlfriend discovered the messages I left and confronted him about his gay affair. Apparently, you had the wrong number printed on those cards, so you may want to change that.'

We dissolve into hysterics and laugh until the tears run down our faces. When I've calmed down, I shake my head.

'No wonder I never heard back from any jobs. That was £12.50 wasted.'

He grins and then I remember Dick and Gina.

'So how come my sister and her porn star boyfriend are here. What's the story there?'

Liam laughs. 'I rang your parents after Mickey hung up and asked if you were still there. They told me you had left the day before so I asked for your number. Your mum was a little unsure whether she should give it to me, so gave me Gina's instead. When I called her, she told me you had gone home and then between us we worked out this little surprise.'

My mind is still whirring and I am finding it hard to take everything in.

'But why all this? I get you needed a date for tonight, and of course, I'm happy to oblige. But this is all so extreme.'

Now Liam looks unsure of himself and looks a little lost if I'm honest.

'Because I don't want you to be my Christmas girlfriend anymore. Gina told me that you felt you couldn't ever compete with April. She said you had zero self-confidence after what had happened and would always feel second best. I wanted to show you that you are far more beautiful than April could ever wish to be. Her image is carefully orchestrated by others. She is made up and styled how others want her to be. She has no personality and is always looking for the next best thing. She doesn't know how to let loose and enjoy herself and every part of her life is stage-managed. I wanted you to feel sexy and confident when you came here today. The photos are to prove to you that you are every bit as beautiful, if not more so than her. I want you to know you are the most beautiful, sexy, woman that I have ever met and I don't want to pretend anymore.'

I can't quite believe what I think Liam is about to say and wonder if I'm dreaming all this. His eyes soften and he looks deep into my eyes.

'I want you to be my proper girlfriend, Annie. I love the fact that you are not only beautiful but kind-hearted and full of fun. You make me laugh and you rock my world. I can't stop thinking about you and if you aren't in my life then I'm not complete. Please say you feel the same?'

I open my mouth but no words come out. I try again and still I can't form words. Liam laughs at the expression on my face and leans towards me.

'I'm just going to take that as a yes. You can't back out now because I've called it. You are now my girlfriend whether you like it or not.'

I lean towards him and whisper.

'You sure took your time – boyfriend.'

Then no more words are necessary as he pulls me towards him and officially kisses the life out of my lips.

Chapter Forty-One
Three Months Later

'What are your plans this weekend?'

I look at Rebecca as she hands me the Pilkington accounts. 'I'm meeting Liam straight from work and we're heading down to Dorset for my Gran's wedding.'

Rebecca raises her eyes. 'Your GRAN'S wedding. Wow!'

I laugh. 'Yes, it's a bit unorthodox, but if you knew my Gran you wouldn't be surprised.'

Rebecca looks impressed. 'Gosh, there's hope for me after all.'

I laugh as I say my goodbyes.

As I head back to my desk, I still can't quite believe how things panned out. Liam and I became joined at the hip and now live together in his minimalistic flat in Notting Hill. We're some kind of cool couple, visiting bars and cafes on our days off and loitering around Art galleries at the weekend. He is still Vogue's number one photographer, but I don't care about that. He makes me feel desired and loved and I couldn't love him more.

I started work at Harris and Goldstein where Rebecca and I clicked over our mutual hatred of Mackinlay- Sanderson.

I love working here, it's everything I dreamed of finding and I'm so grateful to Gail.

She is still with Alex and they make a sweet couple. Tosser moved on, luckily, and took a job in Kingston for a rival Insurance Company. It would appear they have a larger office with lots of fresh talent to corrupt.

Heading down in the lift, I think about the weekend ahead and groan inwardly.

Gina and I are bridesmaids and Gran has chosen the most unsuitable dresses for us to wear. I think she bought them from Ann Summers online. Gina will feel at home wearing it though.

They got the deposit for their flat from sales of their porno on the dark web. Apparently, they are making a sequel to pay for their wedding. I try not to think about it if at all possible, hearing it was bad enough.

The lift reaches the ground floor and I spill out with the rest of the workers, desperate to escape London for the weekend.

As I head outside, my heart lifts as I see Liam waiting for me by the fountain. My sexy boyfriend. How lucky am I? He sees me coming and his face lights up. He rushes over and takes my bag and then kisses me relentlessly.

'Hey, gorgeous. You ready for a weekend of crazy fun?'

I laugh and roll my eyes.

'Sure thing boyfriend. Just promise that you won't use the photos of me in my risqué dress against me. Oh, and don't ever show them to your parents.'

Liam laughs and winks suggestively.

Despite our shaky start, I have grown to like Liam's parents. They finally accepted that he wasn't going back to April and when Liam explained what we had done they just saw the humour in the situation. Luckily, they aren't as bad as I thought. It would have been a nightmare if we hadn't got on.

We head towards the station to grab our train to Dorset.

As we walk hand in hand, I say, 'Hey, you did remember to re-stock the brandy flask, didn't you?'

Liam laughs and pats his man bag.

'All present and correct and filled to capacity.'

'Thank goodness for that. I will need every drop of it to get through this weekend. You do remember what you're in for, don't you?'

Liam grins. 'I wouldn't miss it for the world. I've missed your crazy family and I hope they don't disappoint.'

I laugh and then grin at him. 'I wonder if Elliott will bring Barbie with him.'

It turned out to be Elliott who swapped blow-up Barbie for the sweet wrapper. My Aunt and Uncle were called into the school after he tried to get Macie Green to kiss him in exchange for it. Her parents were horrified when she brought it home and said that a boy had given it to her in return for, 'doing it' with him in the playground. Sounds like one of Delilah's problems.

Mum and Dad are still the same. I've had many a Skype call from them, consulting me over the wedding preparations and deploying me to Selfridges or John Lewis to pick up much-needed stuff for the big day. Mum has gone overboard as usual and I know it will be the most beautiful wedding because of it.

Liam is going to take the photographs, hopefully not like the lady wanted who parted with Barbie.

That was the most embarrassing afternoon of my life, as I assisted Liam when he took the adult photographs.

I don't know how he could even look through the lens at them. I just focused on a stain on their ceiling for most of it. Imagine going around there for dinner and being faced with pictures of their intimate parts.

We join the crowds of commuters all escaping the city and I hope that we get a seat at least. Apparently, we aren't the only ones heading out of town.

As we wait, my thoughts turn to the last wedding we went to together. Charlotte and Eric separated, and she is now dating a polo player from Surrey. She seems happy and Liam seems to like him, so all is good there.

Eric is still a member of his sex club; which I believe he visits most evenings. Luckily, we have nothing to do with him, which is a very good thing.

The train arrives and we join the stampede for the seats. Luckily, we manage to find our favoured spot by the window and as we sit down, Liam grins. 'So, here we are again. A bit different this time, wouldn't you say?' I raise my eyes. 'In what way?'

He laughs. 'Well, I believe we had quite a deception going on last time. It's all straightforward now. It should be easy this time.'

As we look at each other we grin. I watch as Liam removes the brandy from his bag and unscrews the top.

As he offers it to me, he leans in and whispers, 'So, what shall we do this time, girlfriend? Let's make this interesting.'

As the train pulls out of the station I laugh at the wicked glint in his eye.

'Ok, boyfriend. We've got two hours to get our story straight?'

I take a swig of the brandy and pass it back. This weekend is going to be fun.

The End

Thank you for reading My Christmas Boyfriend.

If you liked it, I would love if you could leave me a review, as I must do all my own advertising.

This is the best way to encourage new readers and I appreciate every review I can get. Please also recommend it to your friends, as word of mouth is the best form of advertising. It won't take longer than two minutes of your time, as you only need write one sentence if you want to.

Have you checked out my website?

sjcrabb.com

Out Now

Victoria Matthews has come a long way since she was known as Vicky Matthews, from flat 23 Roundshaw Towers.

The girl who against all the odds managed to claw her way through school and rise above the expectations of her peers.

She is ruthless, unrelenting and driven. She works hard and has no room in her life for anything else. She has no friends and even her own mother flinches when she visits. Her staff fear her and she rips them apart as though they are candidates for the Apprentice. The one focus in her life is making it to the top and today that dream is about to come true.

There is only one man standing in her way.

Charlie Monroe.

Born with a silver spoon in his mouth he had his future mapped out for him from an early age. He was born to wealthy parents and lived the life others could only dream of. He went to Eton and then Oxford and has never had to try for anything because where his brain fails, his looks win. Loved by everyone and desired by many. Popular with his staff and everyone's friend.

Victoria hates him.

They are both in the running to take over the company where they work when Mr Rowanson retires.
However, to win the company they must complete a set of challenges. One for every day of December and on Christmas Day the winner will be chosen. There is one condition. They must work together and have no other help. Every morning on the stroke of 8 they must open the Advent Calendar to discover their challenge. These challenges will determine the winner and failure is not an option.

This is no ordinary Advent calendar and they are not children. This time its war and the winner takes it all.

Prepare for a special kind of Advent where anything can happen......even the unexpected!

♥

Have You read?

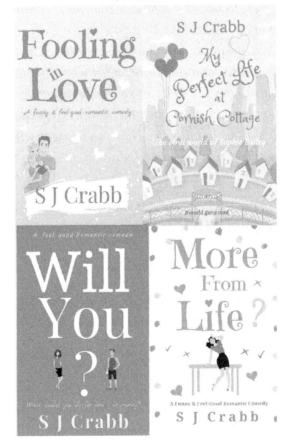

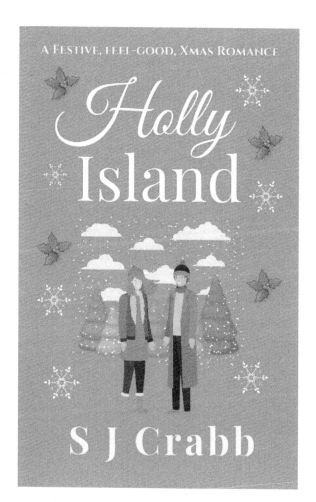

A FESTIVE, FEEL-GOOD, XMAS ROMANCE

Holly

Island

S J Crabb

Buy Now

Made in the USA
Coppell, TX
20 December 2019

13541024R00197